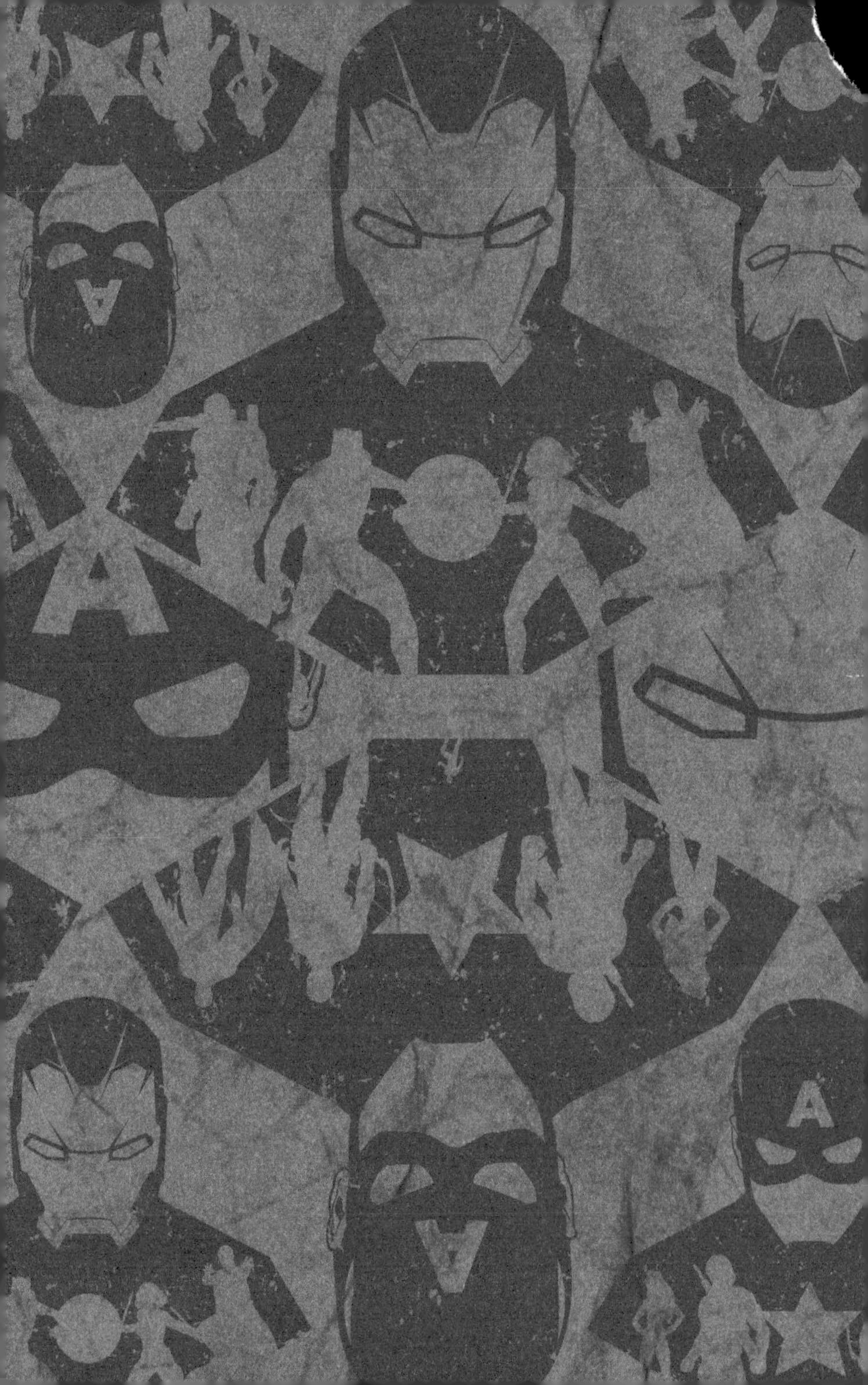

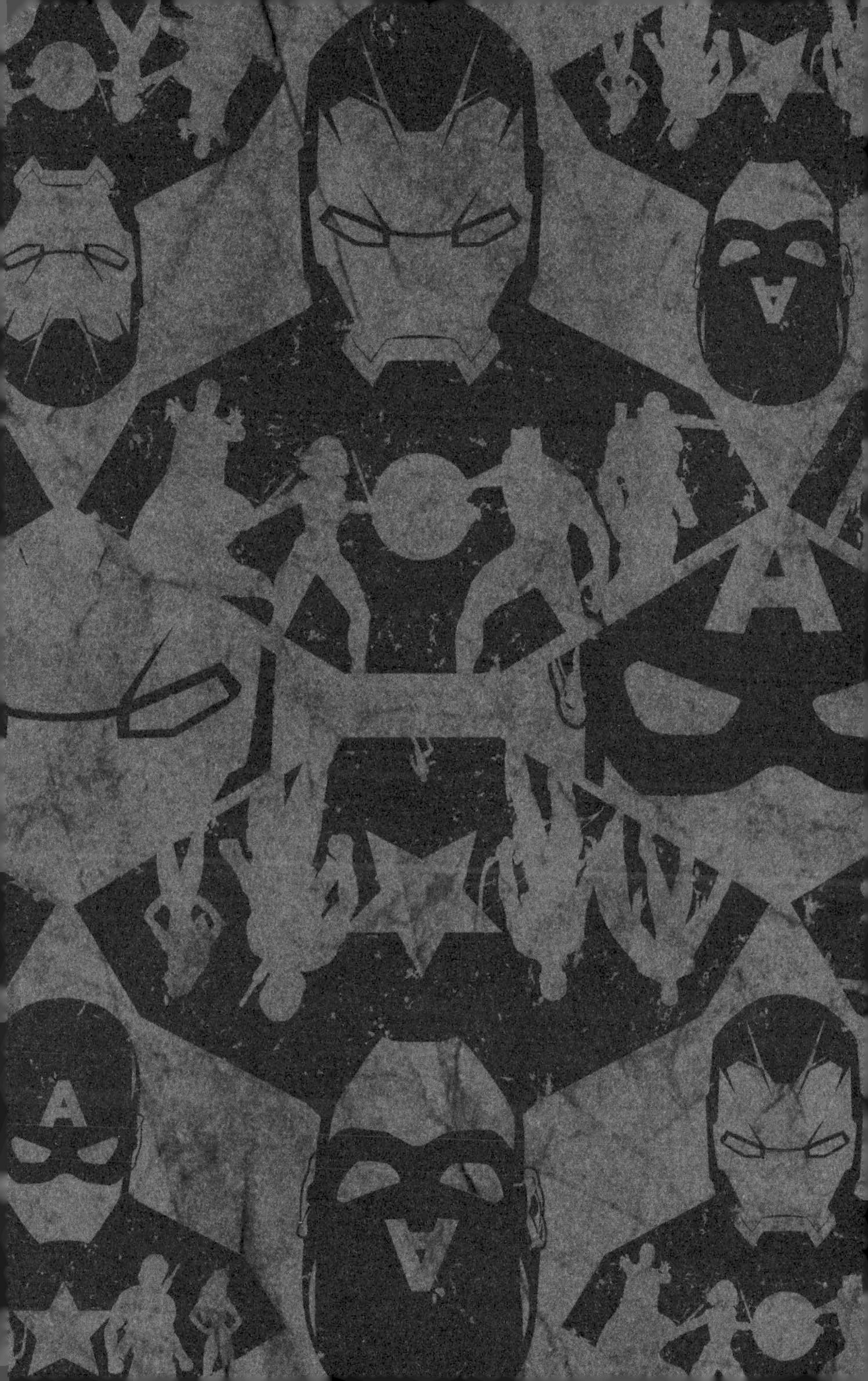

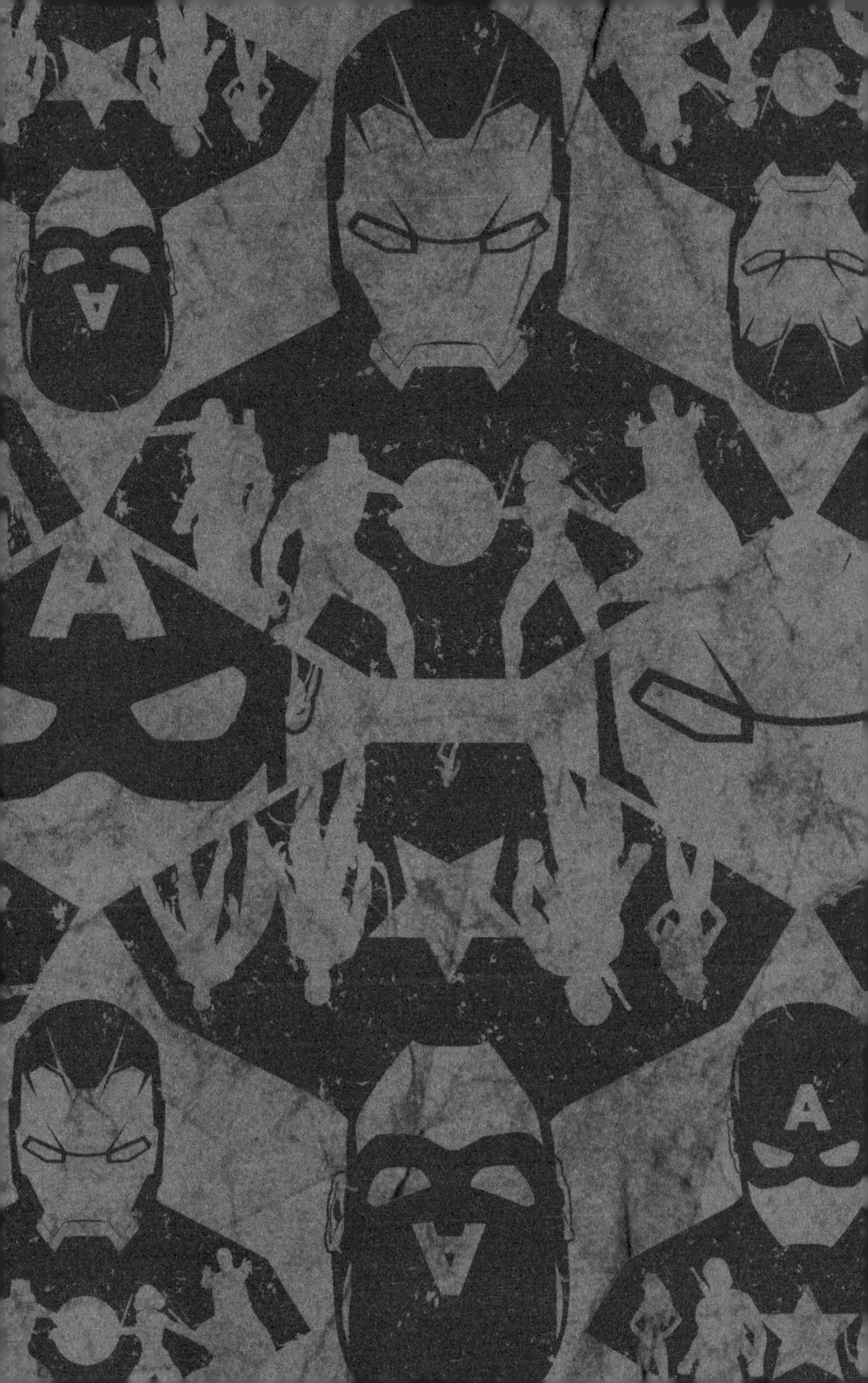

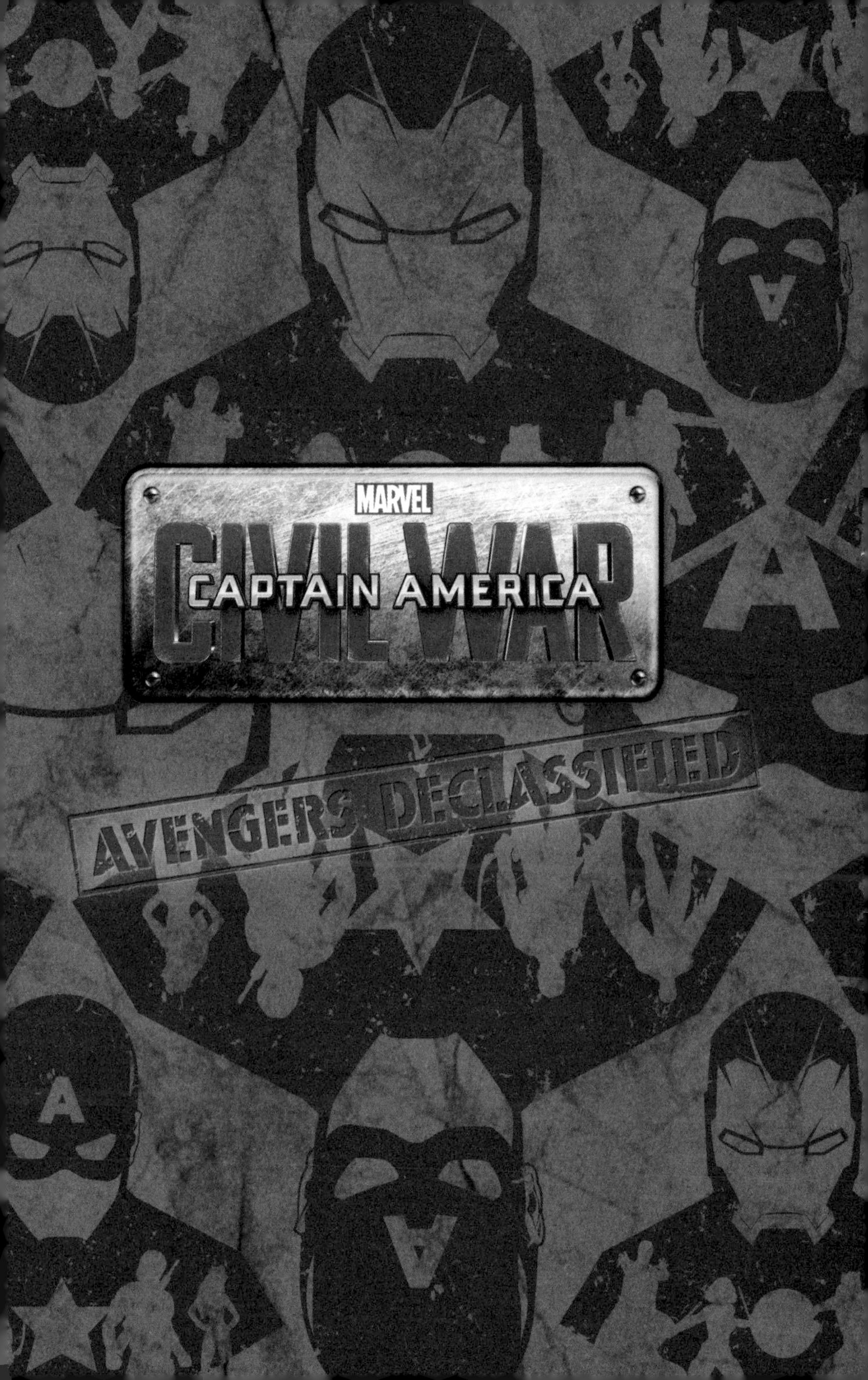
MARVEL
CIVIL WAR
CAPTAIN AMERICA
AVENGERS DECLASSIFIED

marvelkids.com

Little, Brown and Company
Hachette Book Group
1290 Avenue of the Americas, New York, NY 10104

Visit us at lb-kids.com

Little, Brown and Company is a division of Hachette Book Group, Inc. The Little, Brown name and logo are trademarks of Hachette Book Group, Inc.

The publisher is not responsible for websites (or their content) that are not owned by the publisher.

First Edition: April 2016

ISBN 978-0-316-27149-3

10 9 8 7 6 5 4 3 2 1

WOR

Printed in the United States of America

MARVEL

CAPTAIN AMERICA: CIVIL WAR

AVENGERS DECLASSIFIED

OKOVIA ACCORDS

Written by Tomas Palacios
Illustrated by Ron Lim, Andy Smith, and Andy Troy
Based on the Screenplay by Christopher Markus
and Stephen McFeely
Produced by Kevin Feige
Directed by Anthony and Joe Russo

LB
Little, Brown and Company
New York Boston

Following the events in Sokovia, involving
the Avengers' earthshaking battle with
the robotic menace known as Ultron, the
Super-Soldier Steve Rogers, also known
as Captain America, found himself leading
a new team of Earth's Mightiest Heroes.
They operated out of the new state-of-
the-art Avengers Compound.

Captain America's new team—Vision,
Scarlet Witch, Black Widow, Falcon, and
War Machine—continued to respond to global
threats beyond the scope of conventional
authorities, until a new international
law called the Sokovia Accords forced each
Avenger to register with and take orders
from a higher global authority.

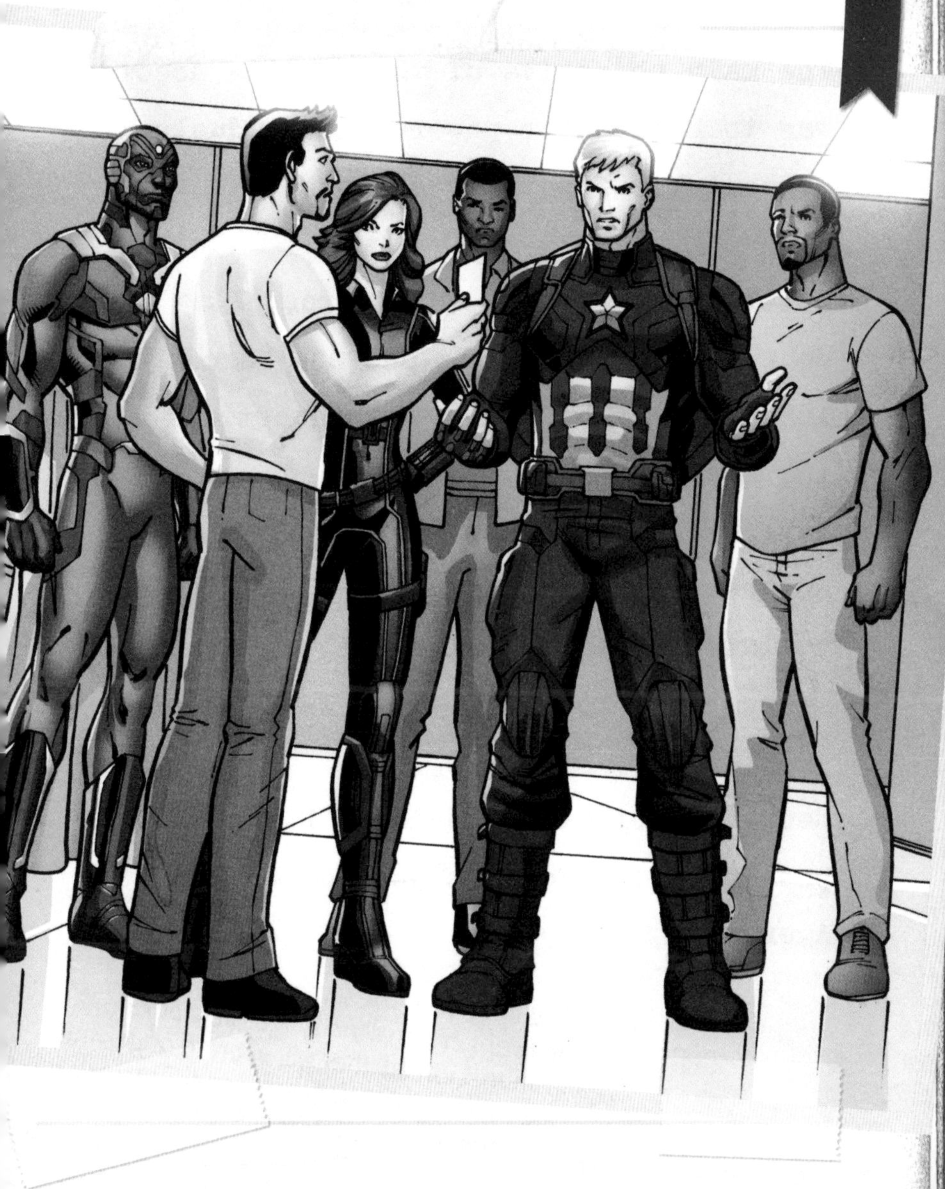

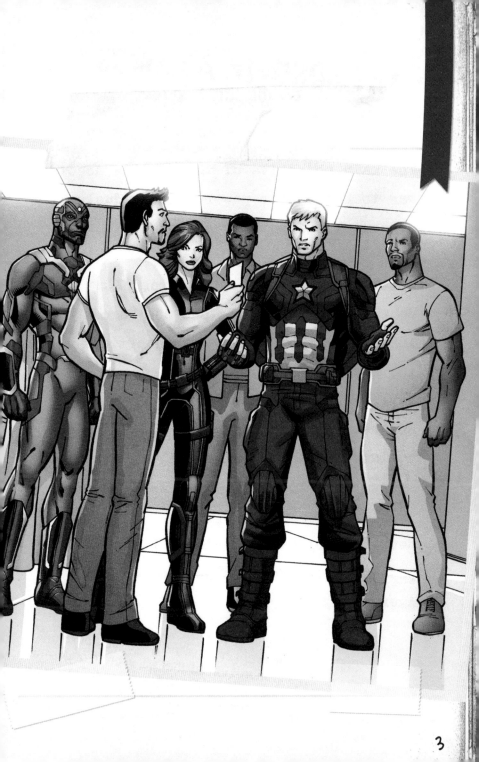

THE SOKOVIA ACCORDS

The main objective of the Sokovia Accords was to hold super-powered individuals accountable for their actions.

After the events in Washington, DC; Johannesburg; Sokovia; and now Lagos, world leaders were left with many questions about the new Avengers, as well as any unreported Super Heroes. How could they prevent another tragedy? How could they prevent collateral damage while still allowing the Avengers to keep the world safe?

Secretary of State Thaddeus E. Ross presented the Sokovia Accords to the Avengers.

Approved by 117 countries, the accords state that the Avengers shall no longer be a private organization. Instead, they will operate under the supervision of a global authority panel. They will act only when and if the panel deems it necessary. ➔

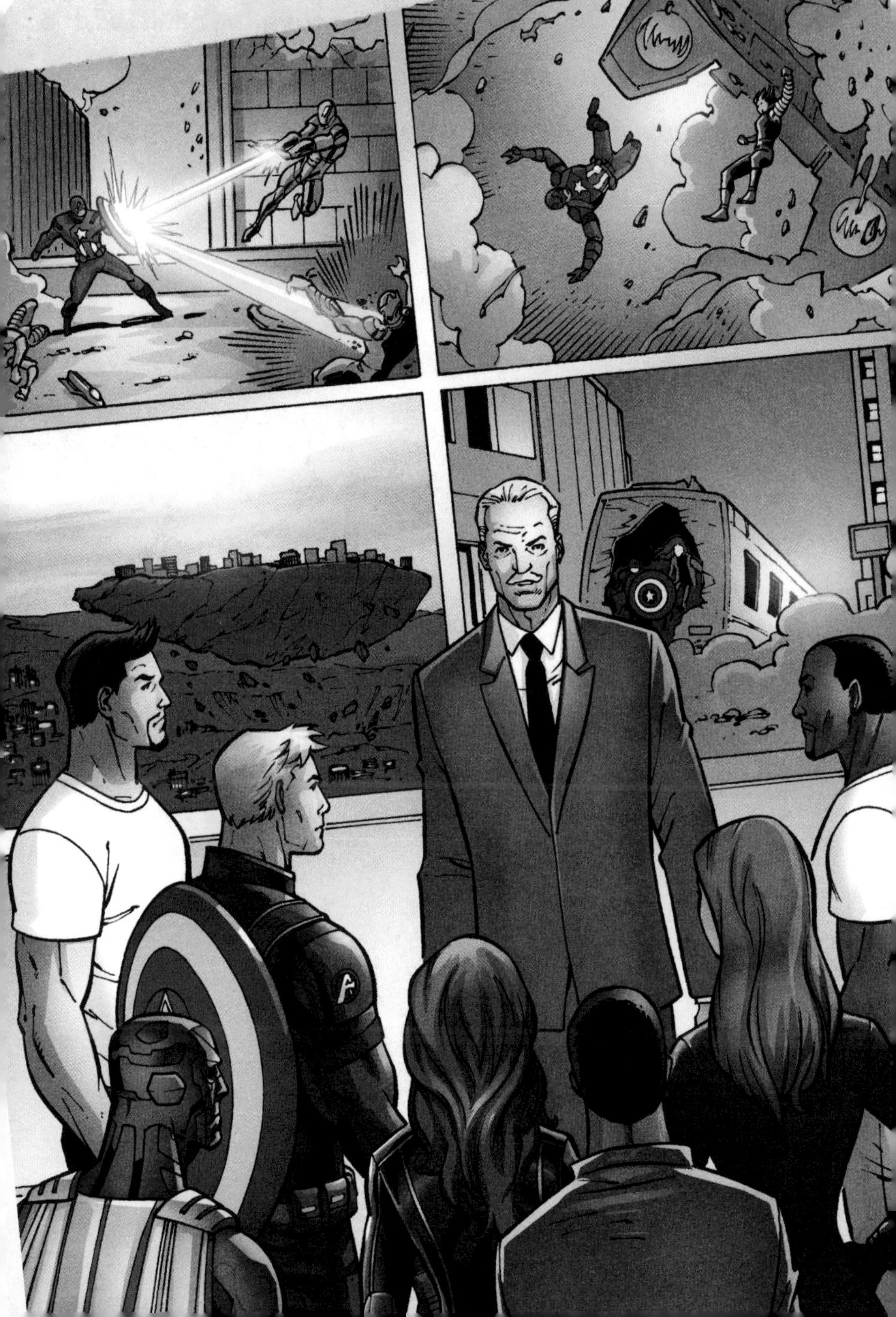

As one would expect, the Avengers were divided. The Sokovia Accords brought conflict and controversy between former allies and teammates.

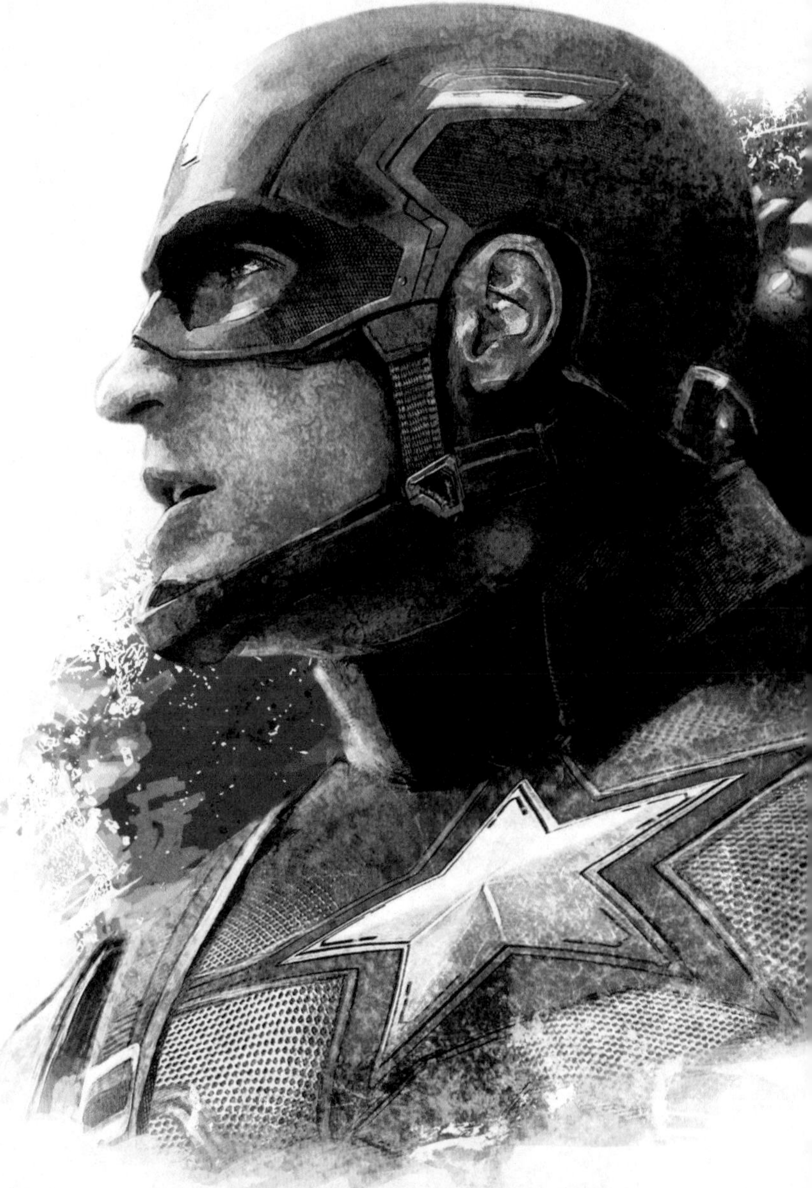

Rallying behind Captain America and his vibranium shield was a faction of heroes who refused to sign the Accords. Cap wanted to operate without regulations; he felt the safest hands were their own. Rallying behind the billionaire tech guru Iron Man was the group of heroes who signed the Accords immediately, knowing that their first mission could be to bring Captain America and other former teammates to justice!

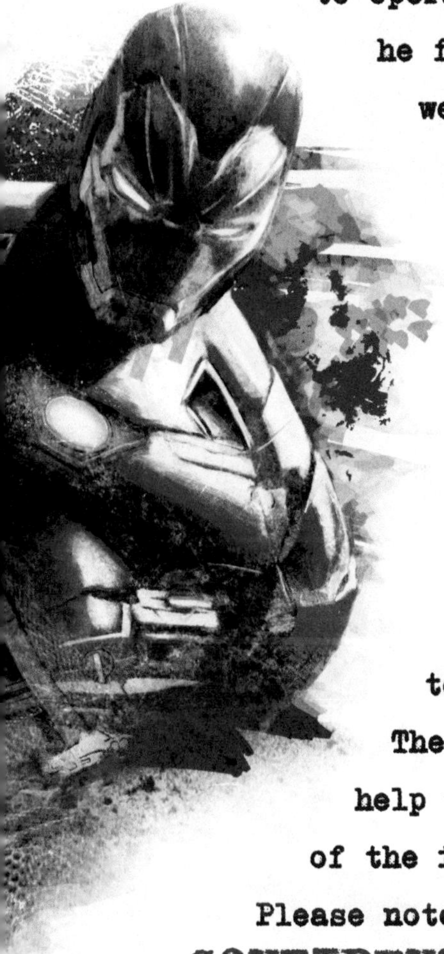

The following records will help to better inform you of the individuals in conflict.

Please note: All intel is highly CONFIDENTIAL and must be destroyed after reading.

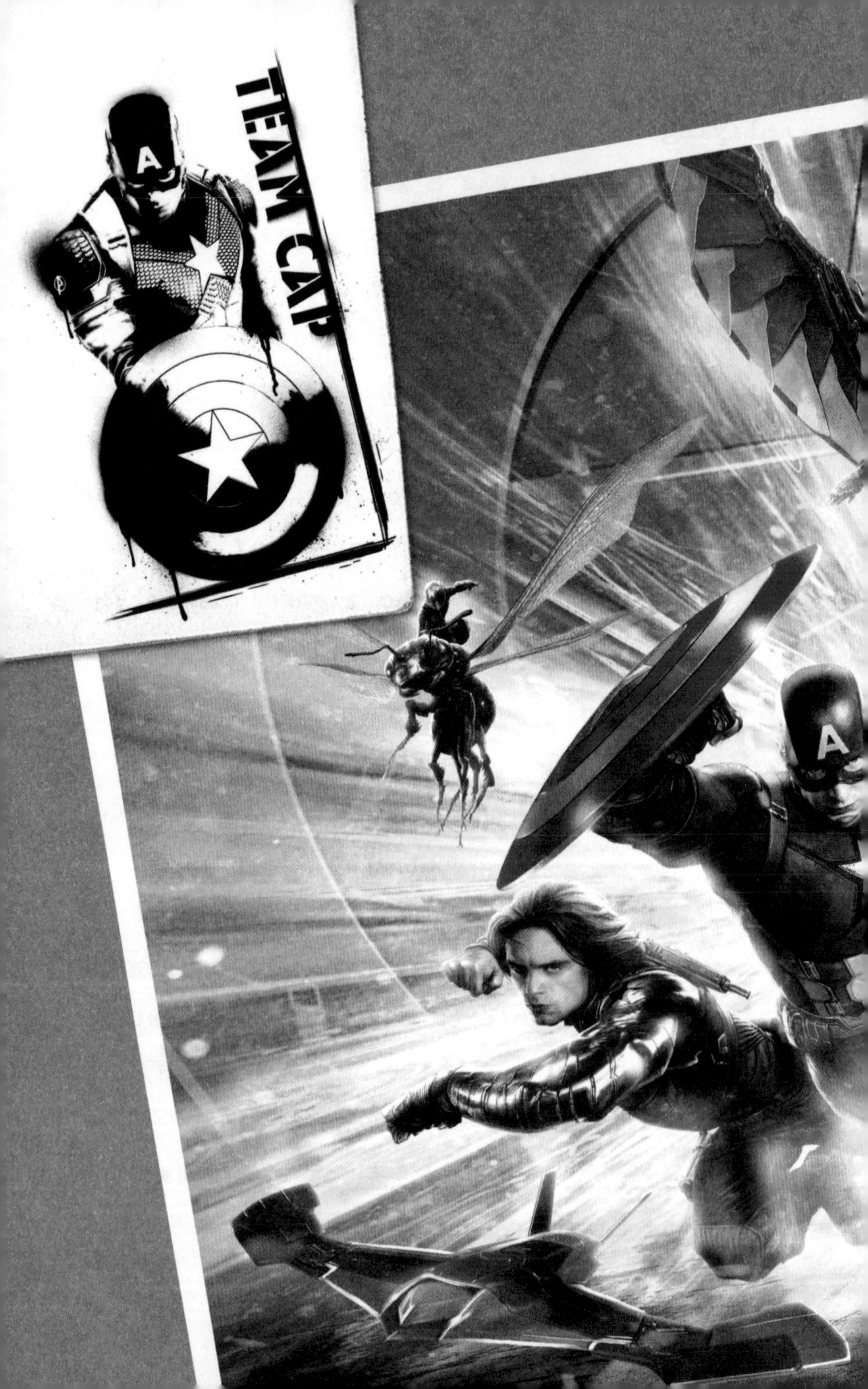
TEAM CAP

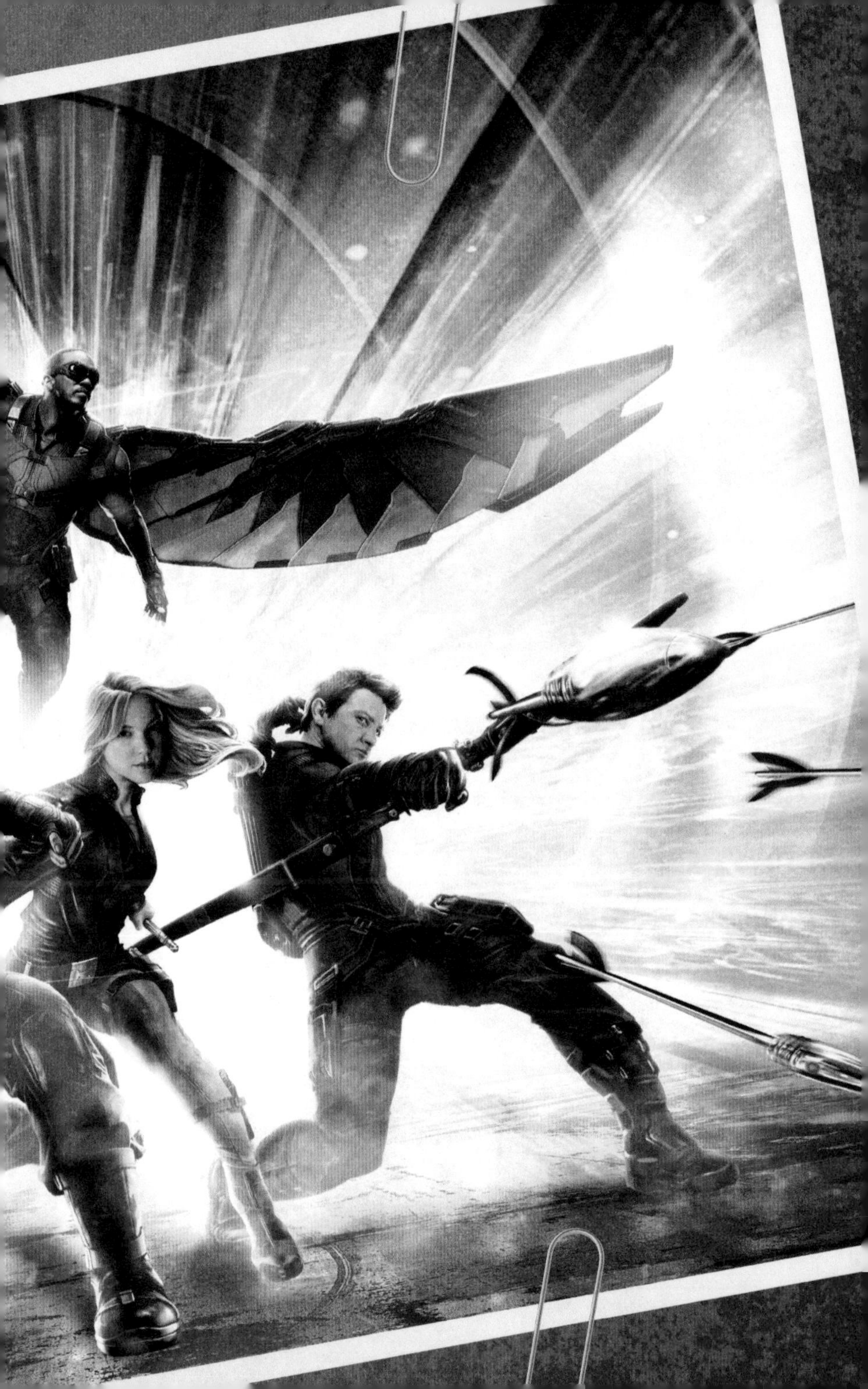

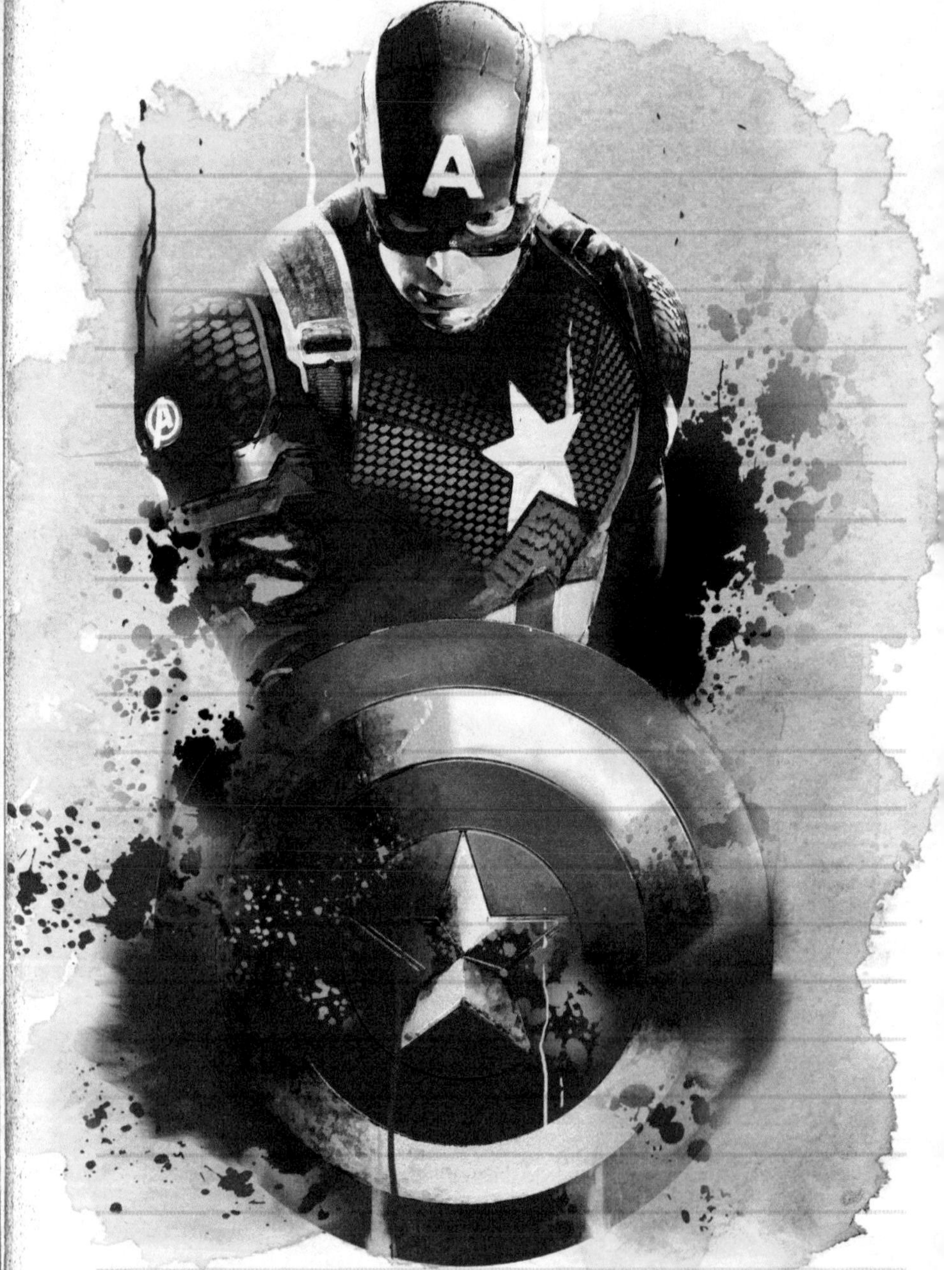

CAPTAIN AMERICA

Augmented by a unique Super-Soldier serum during WWII, war hero Steve Rogers was preserved in Arctic ice for decades. After his revival and reintroduction to modern society, the legendary Captain America found a second calling in life: combating evil and tyranny alongside his fellow heroes as a leader of the Avengers.

CONFIDENTIAL

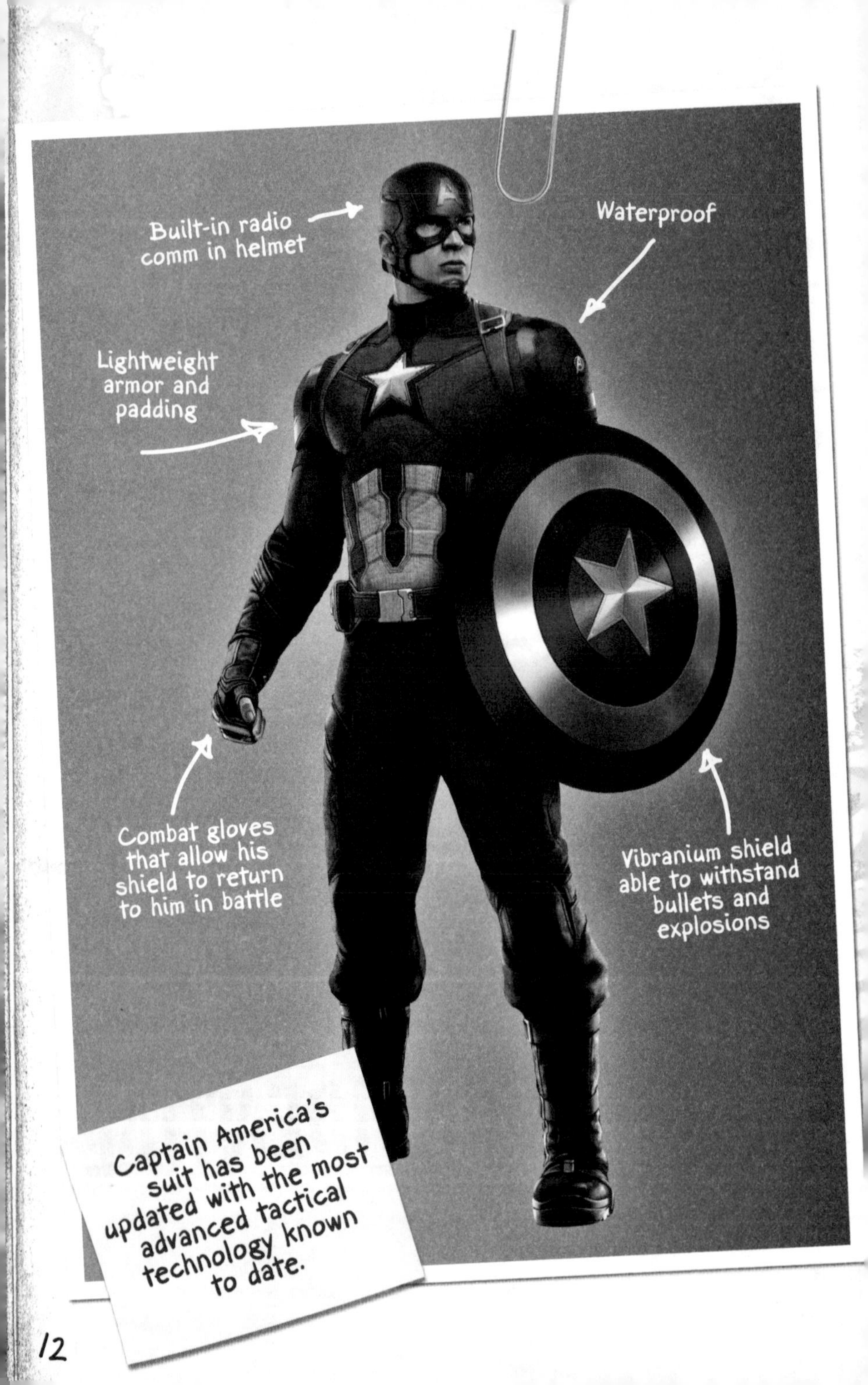
Built-in radio comm in helmet
Waterproof
Lightweight armor and padding
Combat gloves that allow his shield to return to him in battle
Vibranium shield able to withstand bullets and explosions

Captain America's suit has been updated with the most advanced tactical technology known to date.

CAP'S FAVORITE PHRASES

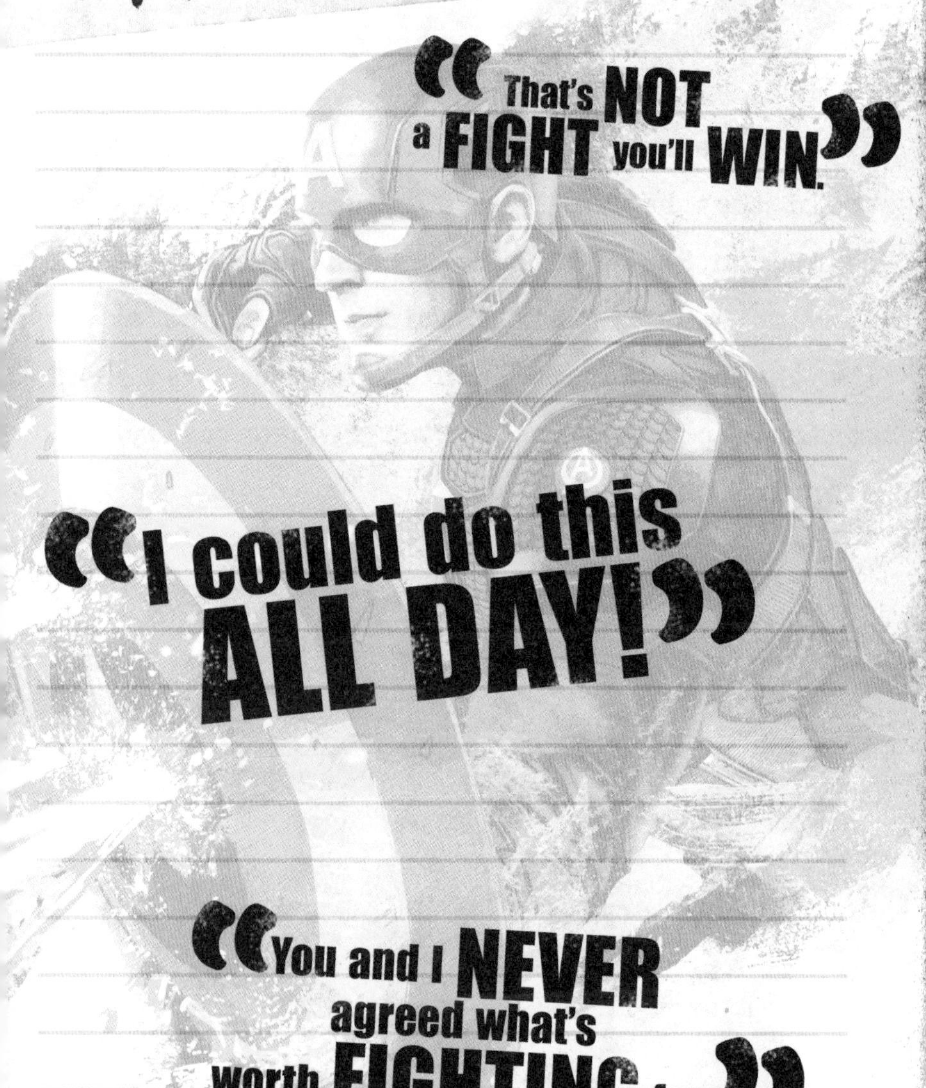

"That's NOT a FIGHT you'll WIN."

"I could do this ALL DAY!"

"You and I NEVER agreed what's worth FIGHTING for."

CAPTAIN AMERICA
HISTORY

Steve Rogers found himself alone in a modern world that he hardly recognized. When Nick Fury called on Steve to suit up and save the world once more as Captain America, he jumped at the chance. Captain America led the Avengers against Loki and the Chitauri, eventually stopping them.

The legendary Cap had returned!

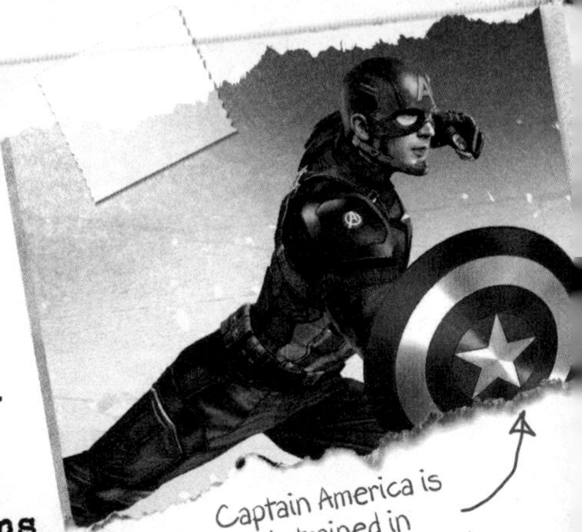

Captain America is highly trained in hand-to-hand combat.

After fighting alongside the Avengers in the Battle of New York, Steve became a dedicated S.H.I.E.L.D. agent and completed many operations with fellow agent Black Widow. Then, alongside Maria Hill and Falcon, they destroyed Project Insight. After the Hydra uprising, Steve went off on his own path to find his long-lost friend Bucky Barnes, who was believed to have died. But Steve was called back to the Avengers and joined the team once again to put a stop to the menace Ultron. After winning the battle in Sokovia, Captain America led the second incarnation of the team.

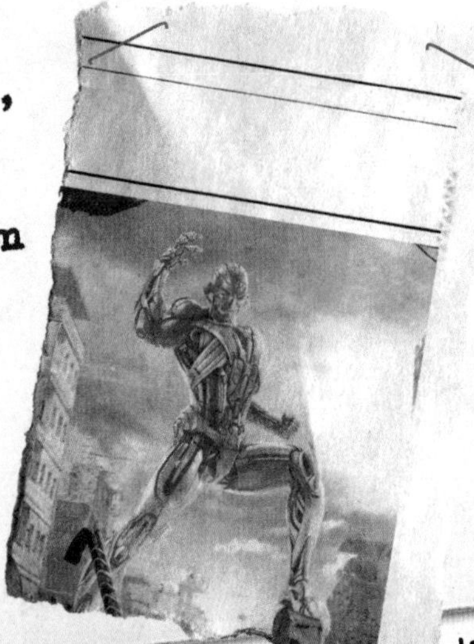

Ultron was a malicious AI with a seemingly indestructible body.

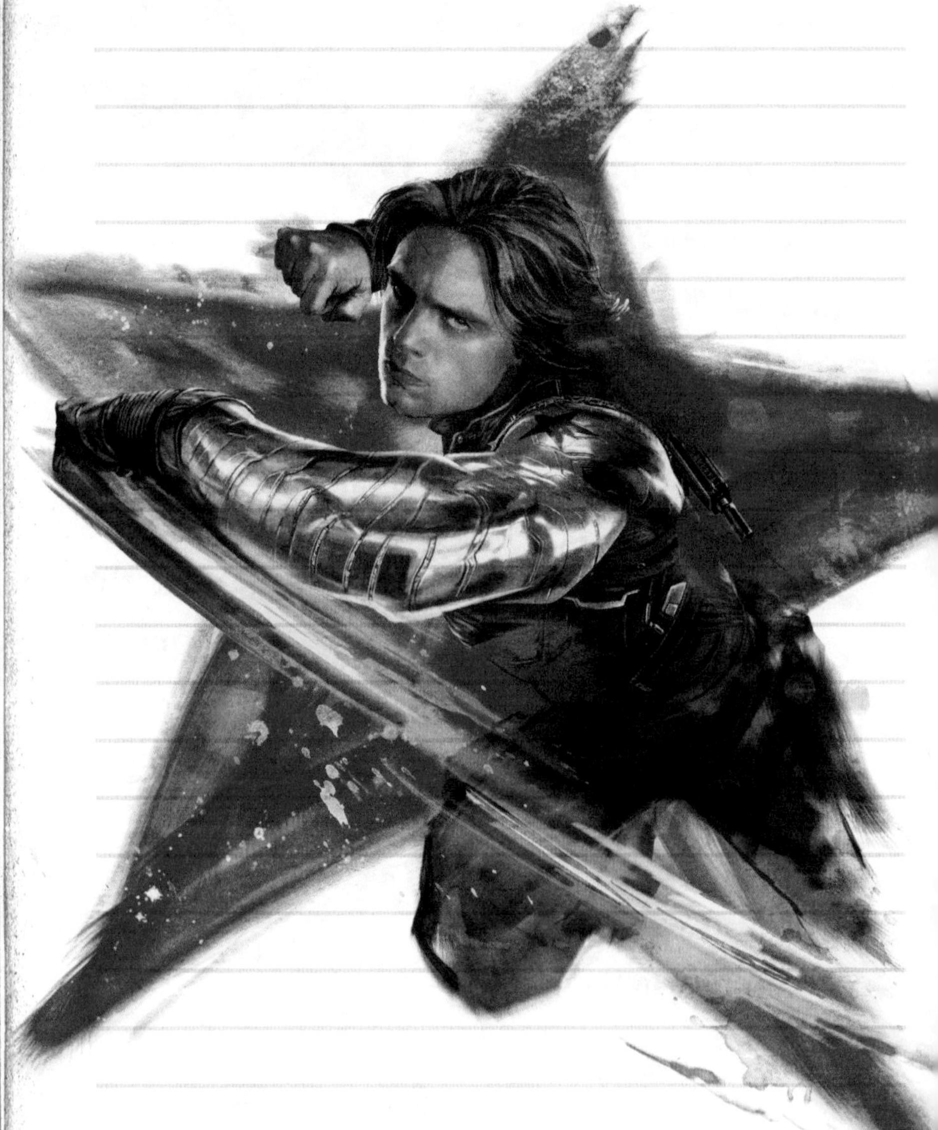

WINTER SOLDIER

Presumed dead after a dangerous WWII mission ended in tragedy, Captain America's childhood friend Lieutenant James Buchanan "Bucky" Barnes was secretly recovered by enemy forces. Subjected to a battery of experiments, Bucky's mind and body were altered, transforming him into the dangerous agent known as the Winter Soldier. Now Bucky seeks to unshackle himself from his conditioning and become his own man.

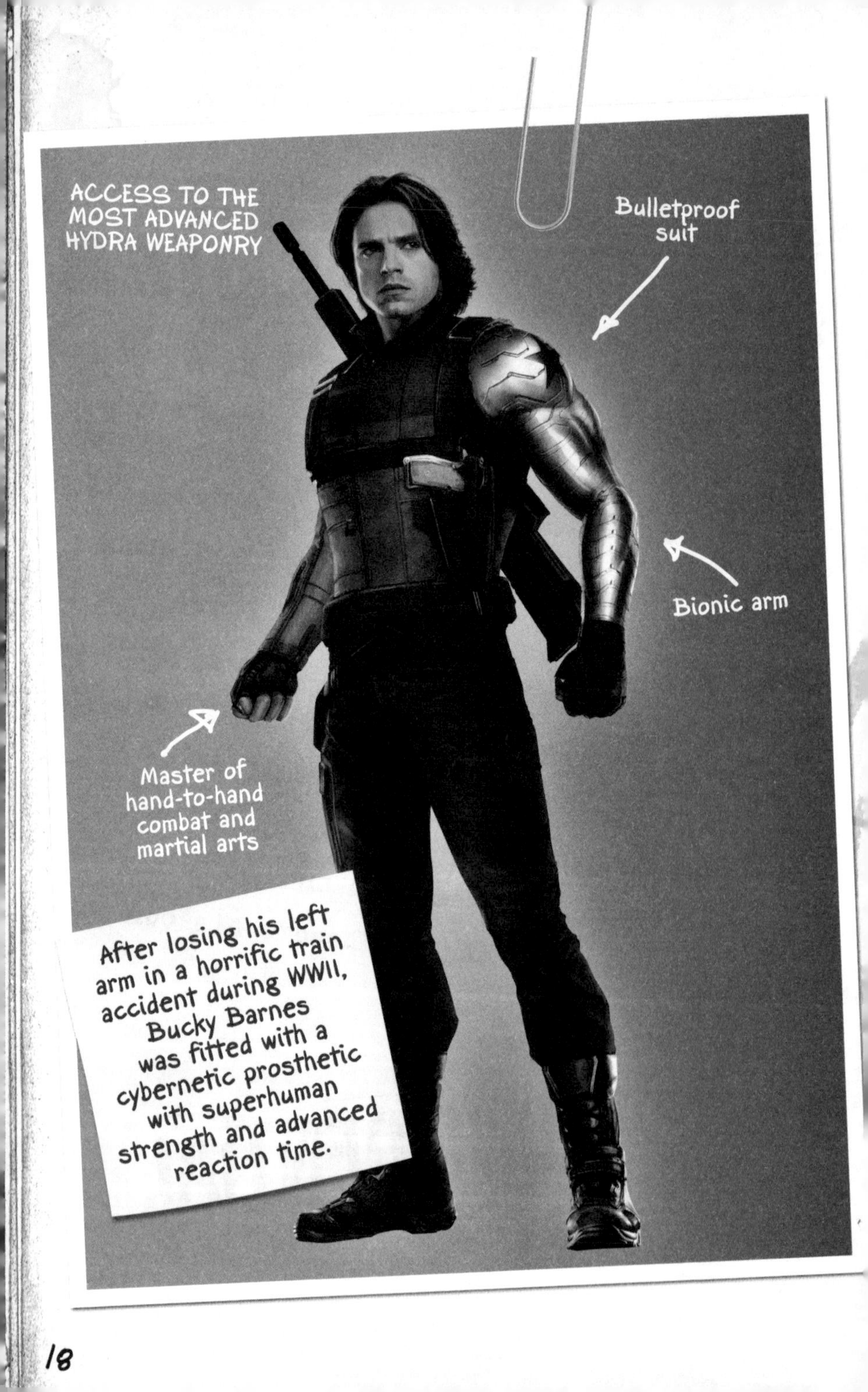
ACCESS TO THE MOST ADVANCED HYDRA WEAPONRY
Bulletproof suit
Bionic arm
Master of hand-to-hand combat and martial arts

After losing his left arm in a horrific train accident during WWII, Bucky Barnes was fitted with a cybernetic prosthetic with superhuman strength and advanced reaction time.

BUCKY'S FAVORITE PHRASES

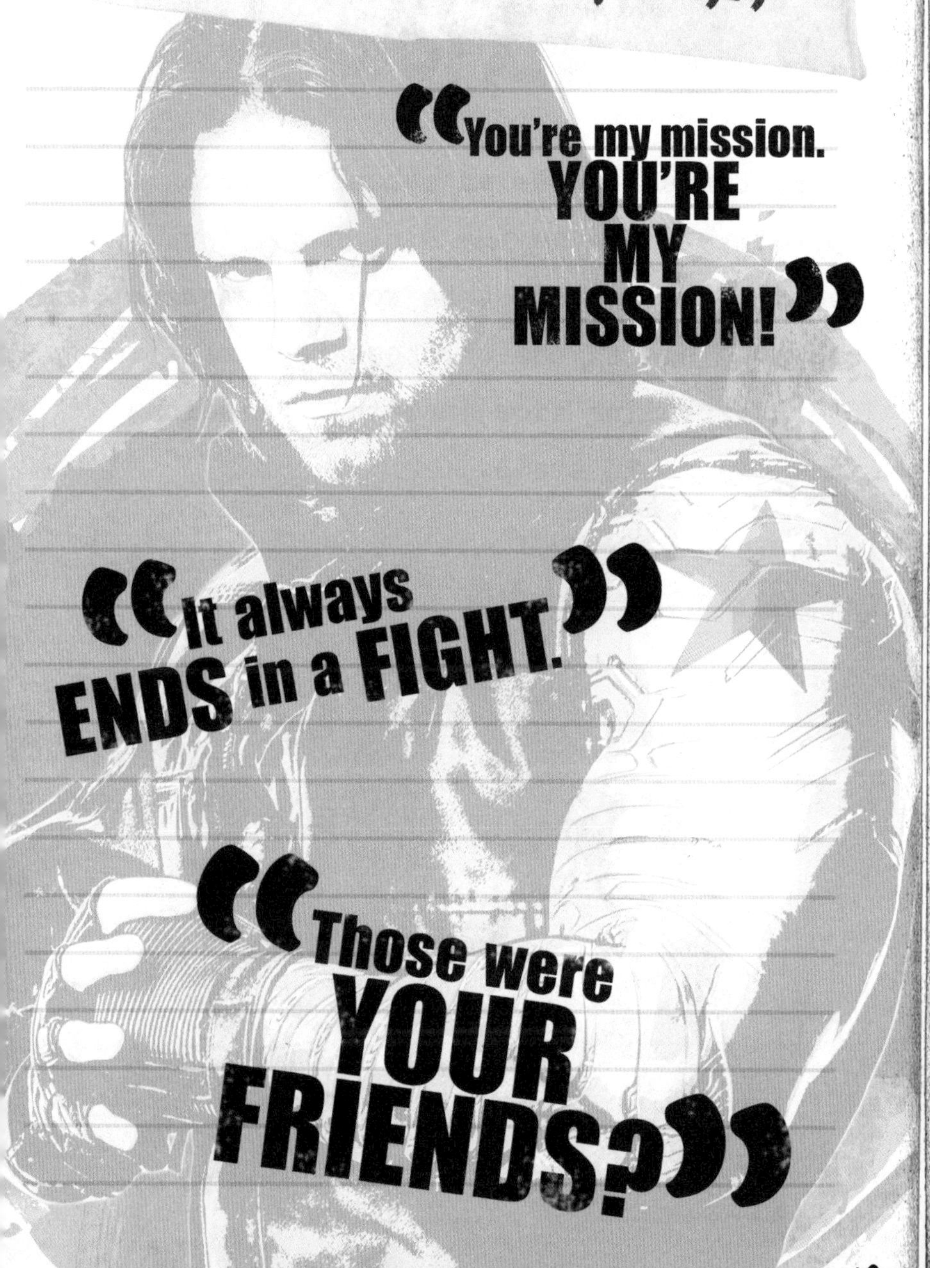

"You're my mission. **YOU'RE MY MISSION!**"

"It always **ENDS** in a **FIGHT.**"

"Those were **YOUR FRIENDS?**"

WINTER SOLDIER
HISTORY

Bucky Barnes became an enhanced Hydra
operative known as the Winter Soldier.
Over several decades, he would assassinate
everyone and anyone who posed a threat to
Hydra, spending time in between missions
in a cryogenic state.

The Winter Soldier
is a top field agent.

He is highly trained in hand-to-hand combat.

However, when he was sent to
kill Nick Fury, director of S.H.I.E.L.D.,
he was confronted by his old friend Steve Rogers,
which jump-started his memory of who he really was.

An epic battle occurred at the Triskelion facility,
where several state-of-the art Hellicarriers were
destroyed, and for good reason, as they were
secretly programmed by Hydra to target large
cities and eliminate millions of innocent lives.

After the events of the battle at the Triskelion
with Captain America, the facility was destroyed
and Bucky appeared to have vanished.

But we now have surveillance of Bucky Barnes
saving his longtime friend Steve Rogers from
the Potomac River before making his escape.

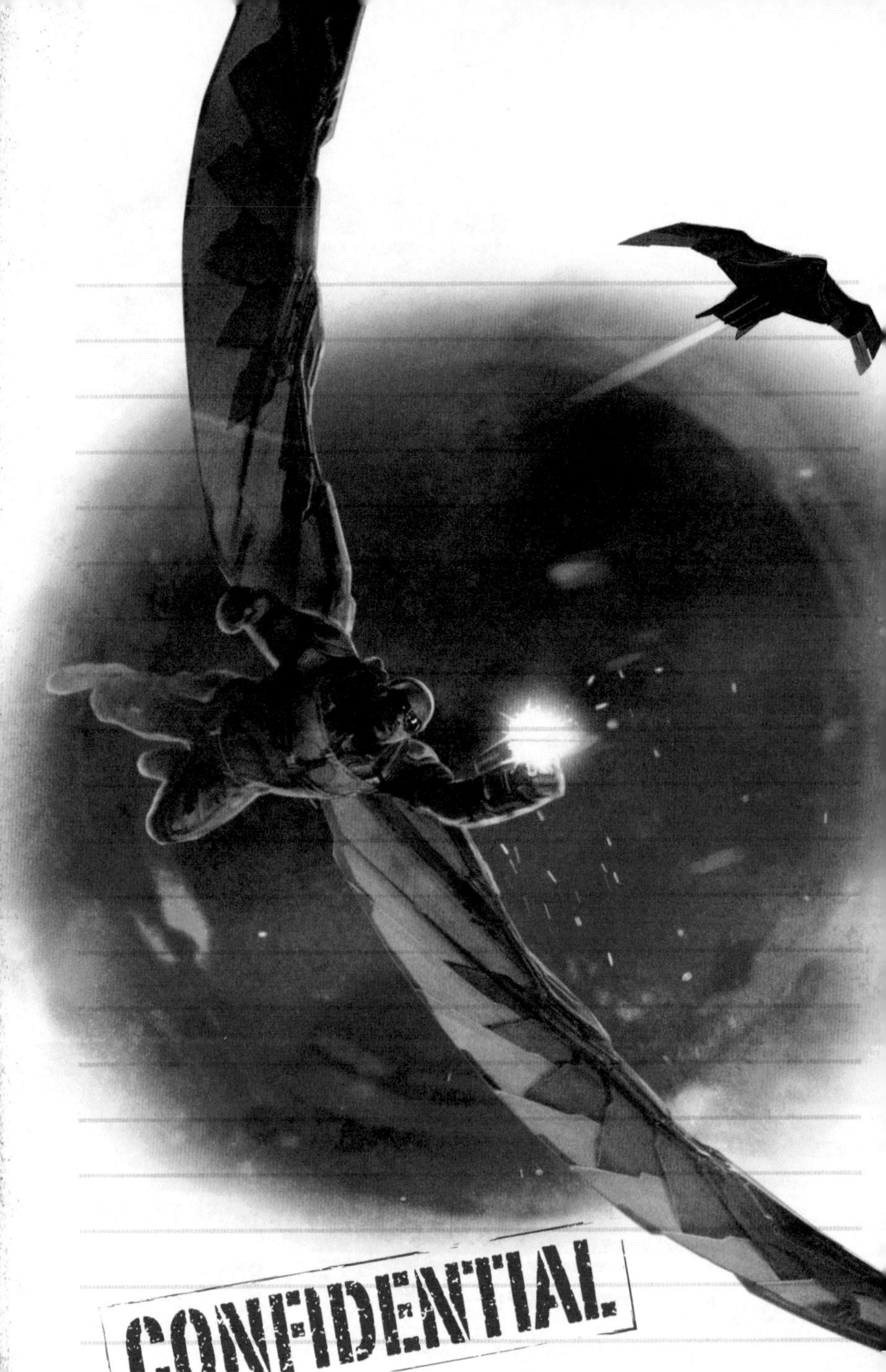
CONFIDENTIAL

FALCON
& REDWING

A former pararescue specialist of the 58th Division, Sam Wilson went on to work with recovering veterans in Washington, DC. He aided the legendary Captain America in adjusting to modern life, quickly becoming Cap's close friend in the process. The two first met jogging around the National Mall in Washington, DC, and immediately became friends, bonding over their experiences as soldiers and how they'd lost many friends on the battlefield. When Cap and Black Widow were in dire need of aid, Falcon did not hesitate to suit up. Using an experimental winged harness, Sam took to the skies as the high-flying Falcon.

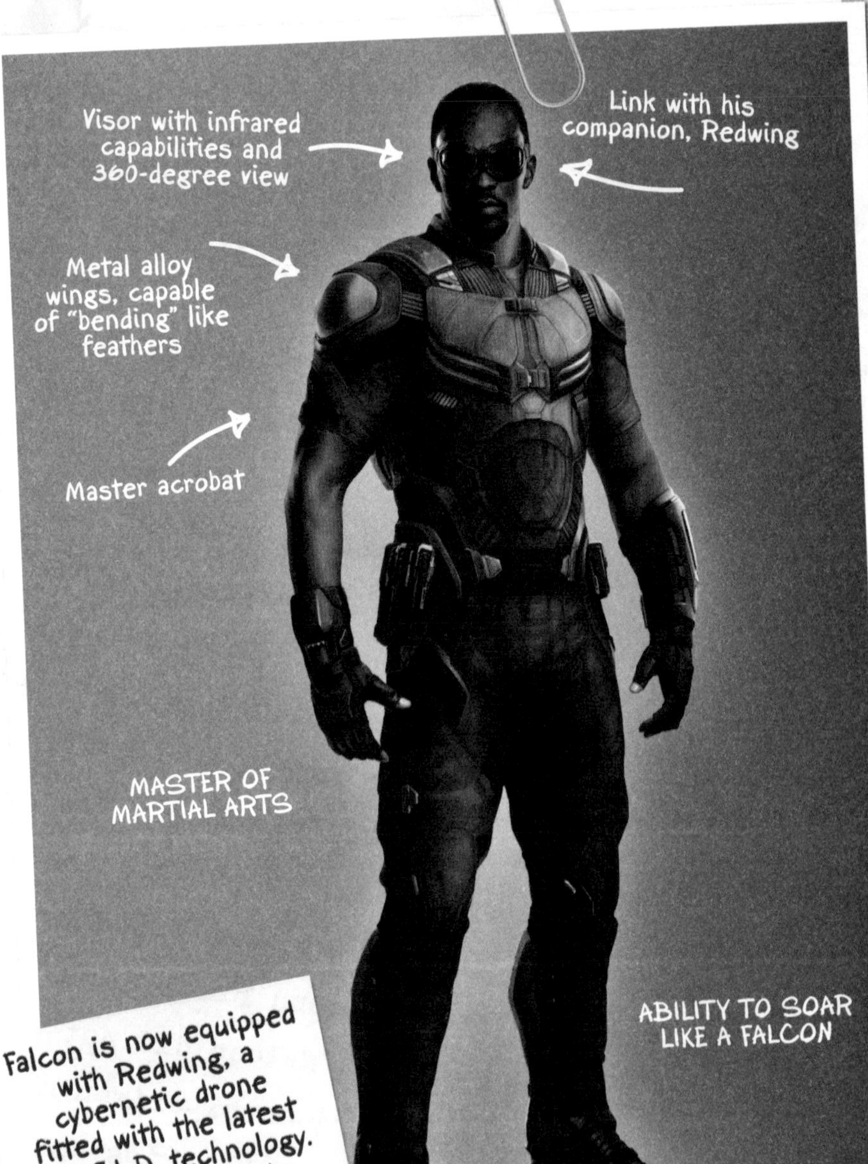
Visor with infrared capabilities and 360-degree view
Link with his companion, Redwing
Metal alloy wings, capable of "bending" like feathers
Master acrobat
MASTER OF MARTIAL ARTS
ABILITY TO SOAR LIKE A FALCON

Falcon is now equipped with Redwing, a cybernetic drone fitted with the latest S.H.I.E.L.D. technology. Redwing is able to support Falcon on missions and tasks where he is "blind."

FALCON'S FAVORITE PHRASES

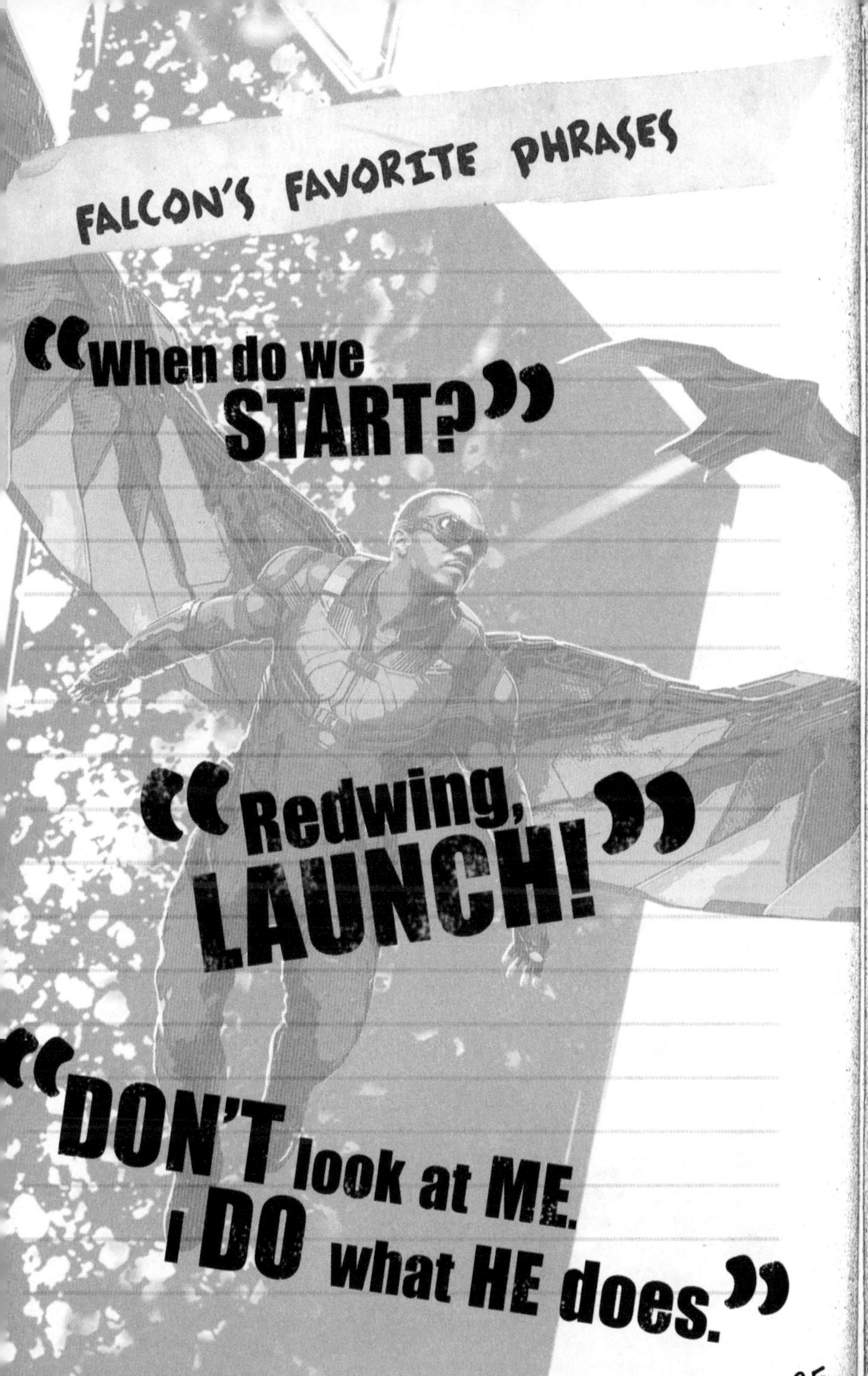

"When do we START?"

"Redwing, LAUNCH!"

"DON'T look at ME. I DO what HE does."

FALCON
HISTORY

Falcon became great allies with Captain
America during the Hydra uprising, after which
he assisted Cap during his search for Bucky
Barnes. After the war against Ultron, Sam
became a member of the second incarnation of
the Avengers. His recent encounter with
Ant-Man at the new Avengers facility led him
to recommend the shrinking hero for Captain
America's newest team, which was fighting
government regulation of Super Heroes.

Falcon has
tactical command
of the skies.

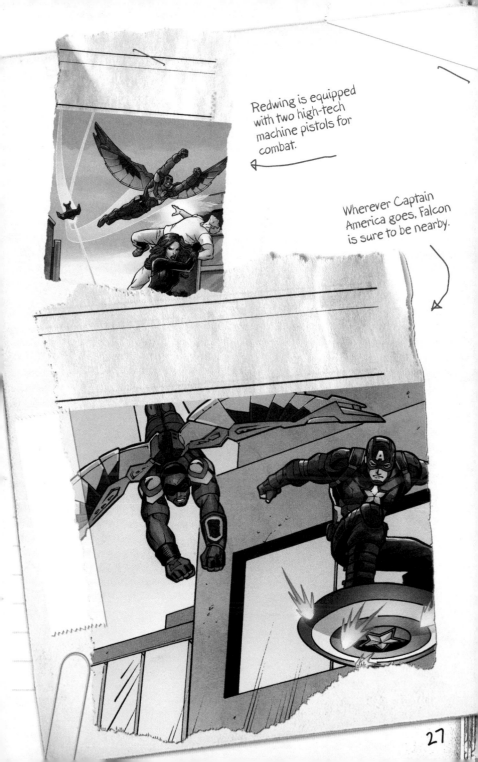

Redwing is equipped with two high-tech machine pistols for combat.

Wherever Captain America goes, Falcon is sure to be nearby.

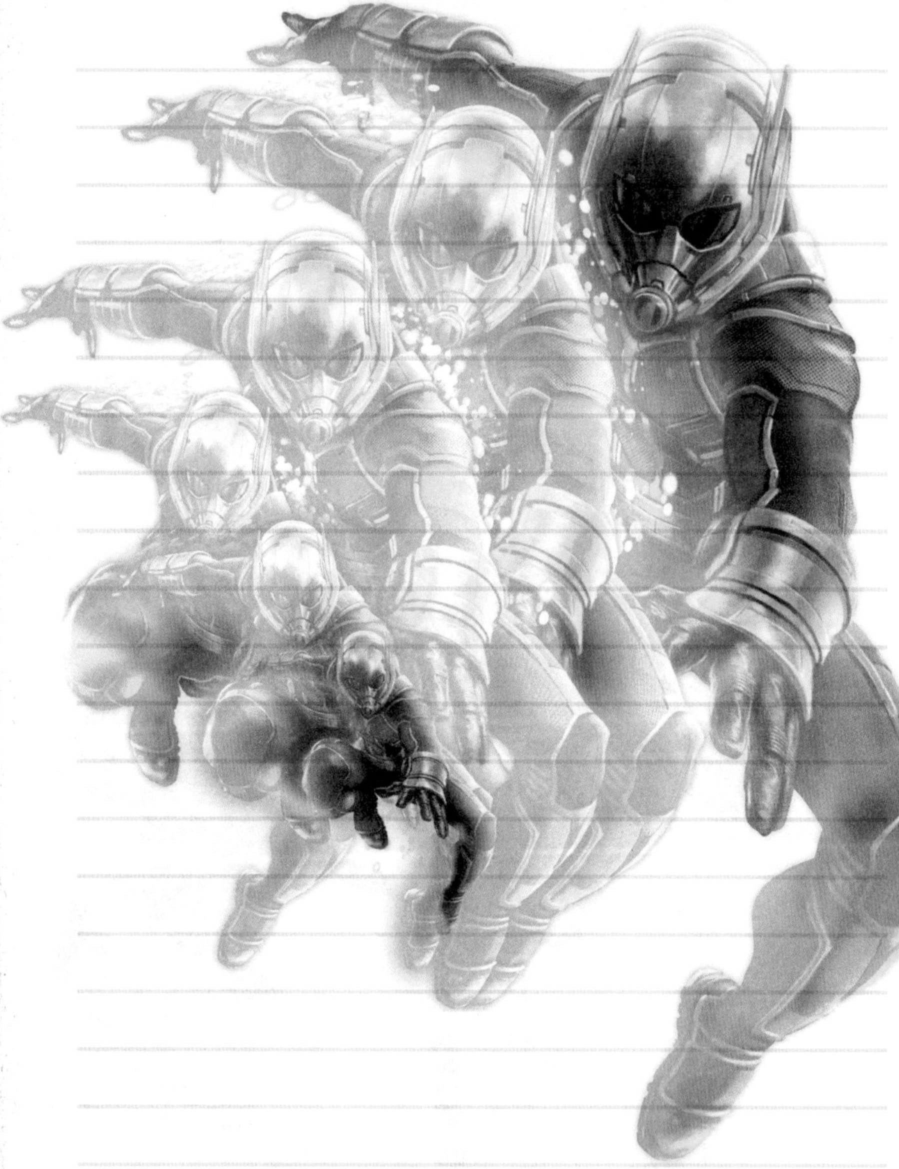

ANT-MAN

A former thief who proved himself a hero, Scott Lang was entrusted with the astonishing Ant-Man suit, a uniquely sophisticated piece of technology that allows him to shrink in size but increase in power. As Ant-Man, Scott is able to handle the jobs "too small" for any other hero.

CONFIDENTIAL

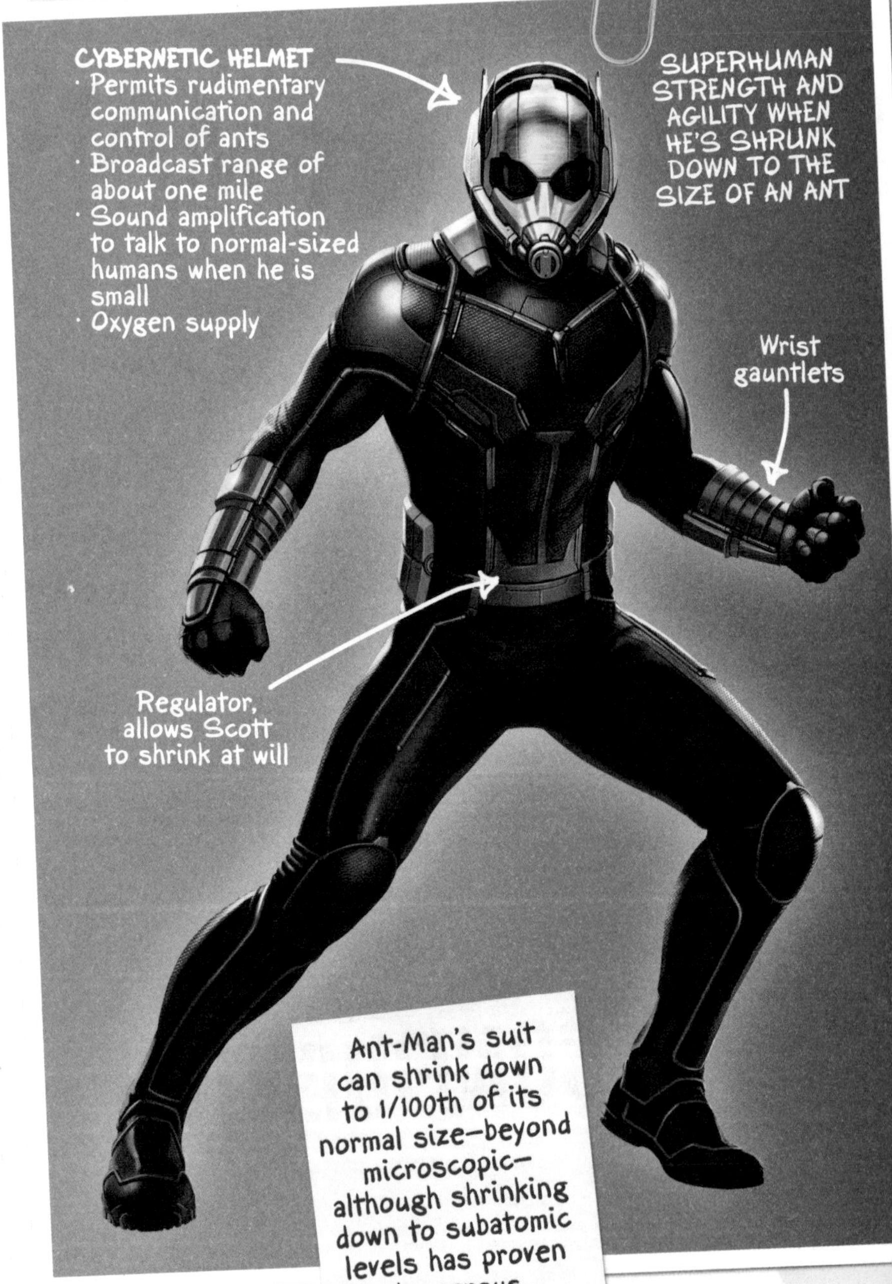
CYBERNETIC HELMET
· Permits rudimentary communication and control of ants
· Broadcast range of about one mile
· Sound amplification to talk to normal-sized humans when he is small
· Oxygen supply
SUPERHUMAN STRENGTH AND AGILITY WHEN HE'S SHRUNK DOWN TO THE SIZE OF AN ANT
Wrist gauntlets
Regulator, allows Scott to shrink at will

Ant-Man's suit can shrink down to 1/100th of its normal size—beyond microscopic—although shrinking down to subatomic levels has proven dangerous.

ANT-MAN'S FAVORITE PHRASES

"THEY may have mentioned something about SAVING THE WORLD."

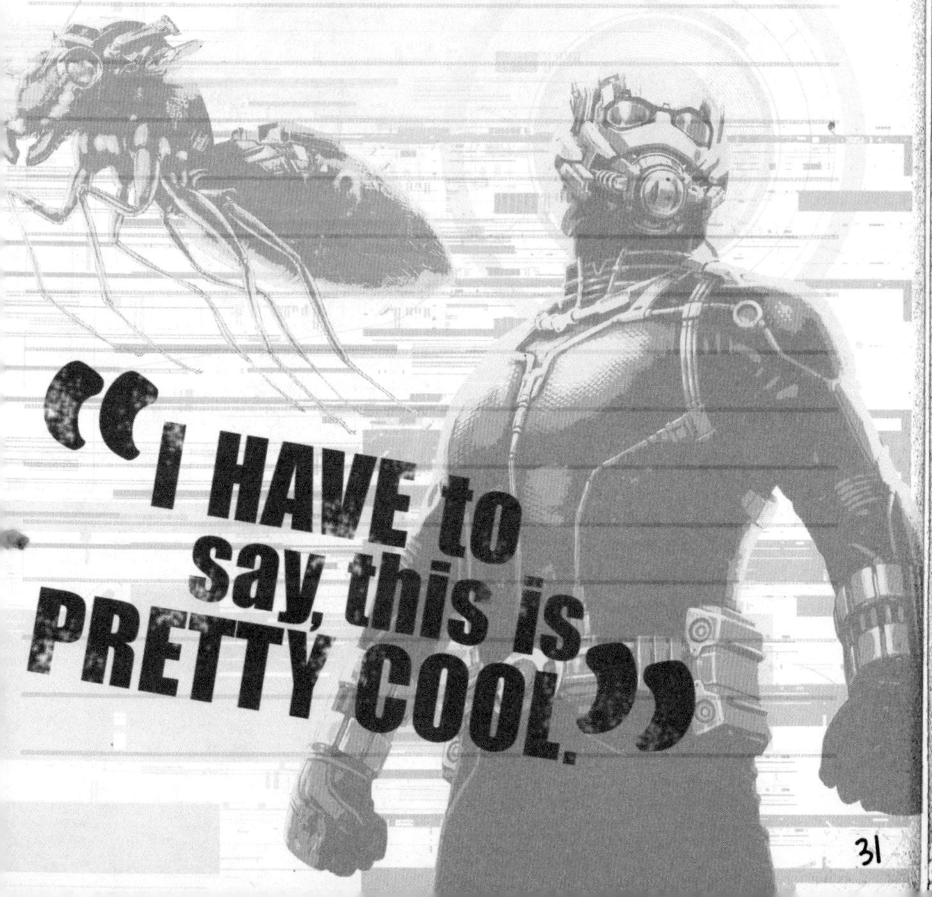

"I HAVE to say, this is PRETTY COOL."

ANT-MAN HISTORY

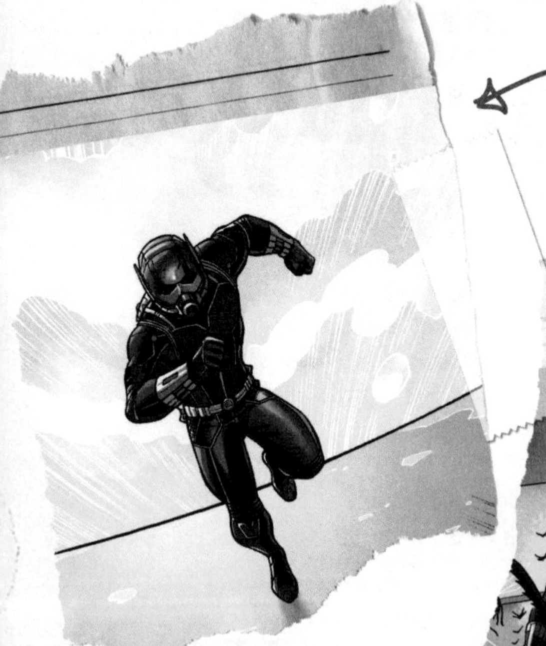

Ant-Man's first time in the suit was a near disaster.

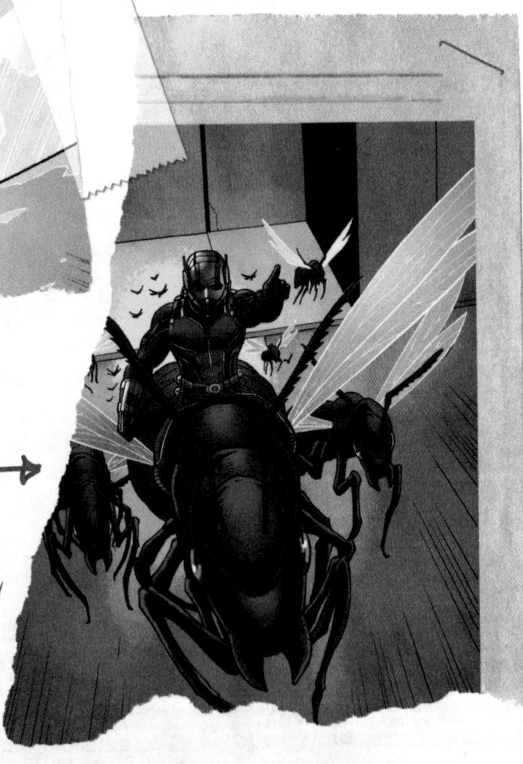

Ant-Man is able to control a wide variety of ants.

Even at small sizes, Ant-Man can take a beating.

Scott Lang became Ant-Man after stealing a suit from the legendary scientist Hank Pym—a suit which gave him the ability to shrink. Instead of prosecuting Scott, Hank took him in and trained him as the all-new Ant-Man, tasking him with stopping the diabolical Darren Cross from turning Pym's technology into a weapon. Along the way, Scott was forced to confront Falcon, who ultimately recommended Ant-Man to Captain America for missions suited to his unique talents.

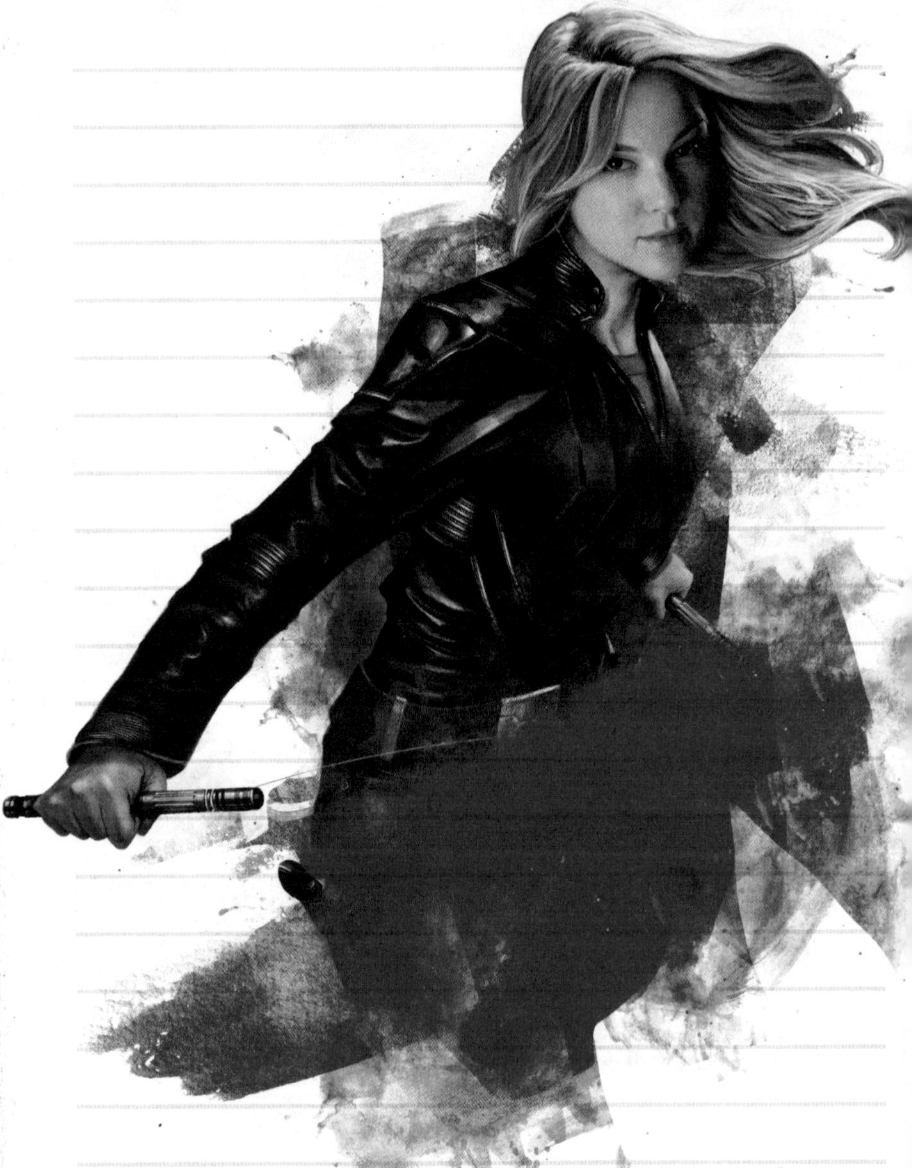

AGENT 13

A talented and loyal member of S.H.I.E.L.D. before its dissolution, Sharon Carter, also known as Agent 13, was originally sent to observe Captain America as he adjusted to modern life. She has since become one of Cap's closest friends and allies, watching his back by using her impressive talents in the art of espionage.

CONFIDENTIAL

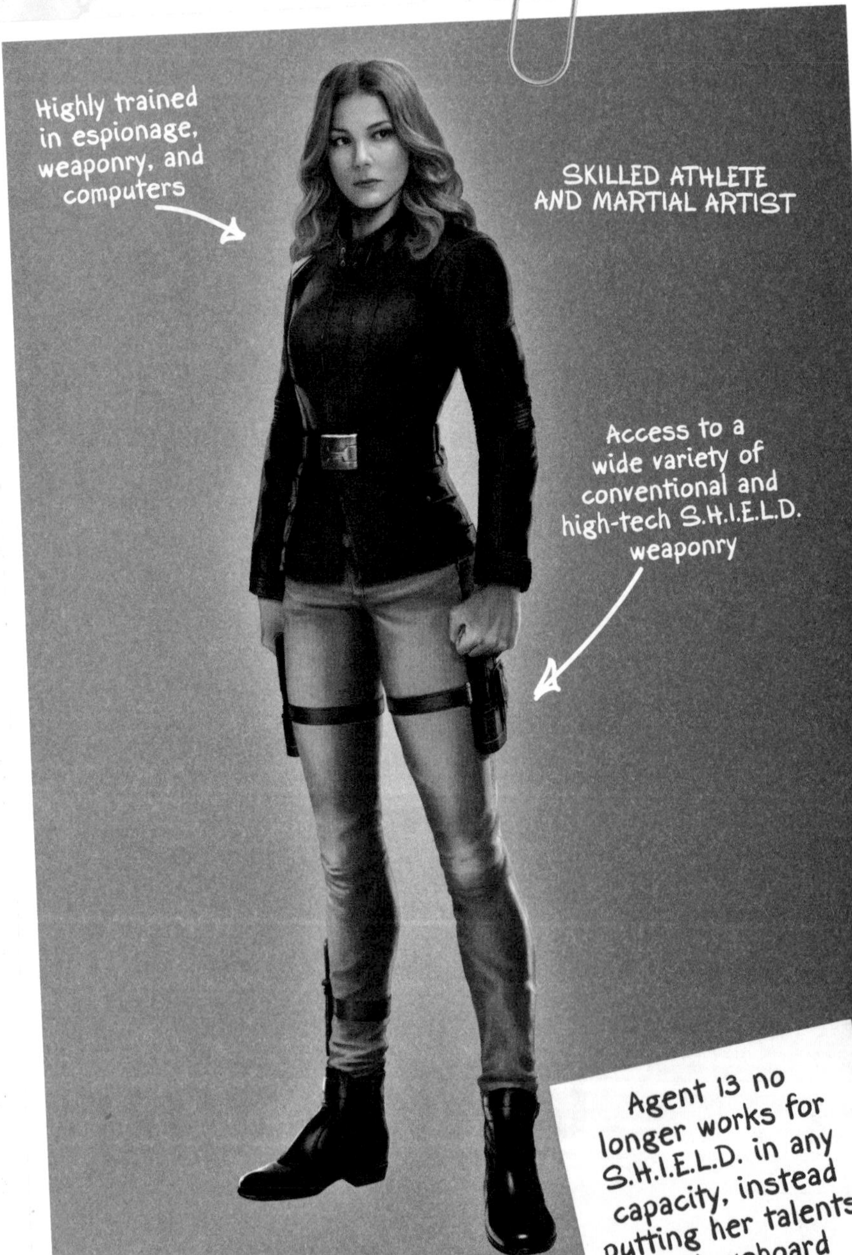

Highly trained in espionage, weaponry, and computers

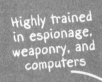

SKILLED ATHLETE AND MARTIAL ARTIST

Access to a wide variety of conventional and high-tech S.H.I.E.L.D. weaponry

Agent 13 no longer works for S.H.I.E.L.D. in any capacity, instead putting her talents to aboveboard government agencies.

AGENT 13'S FAVORITE PHRASES

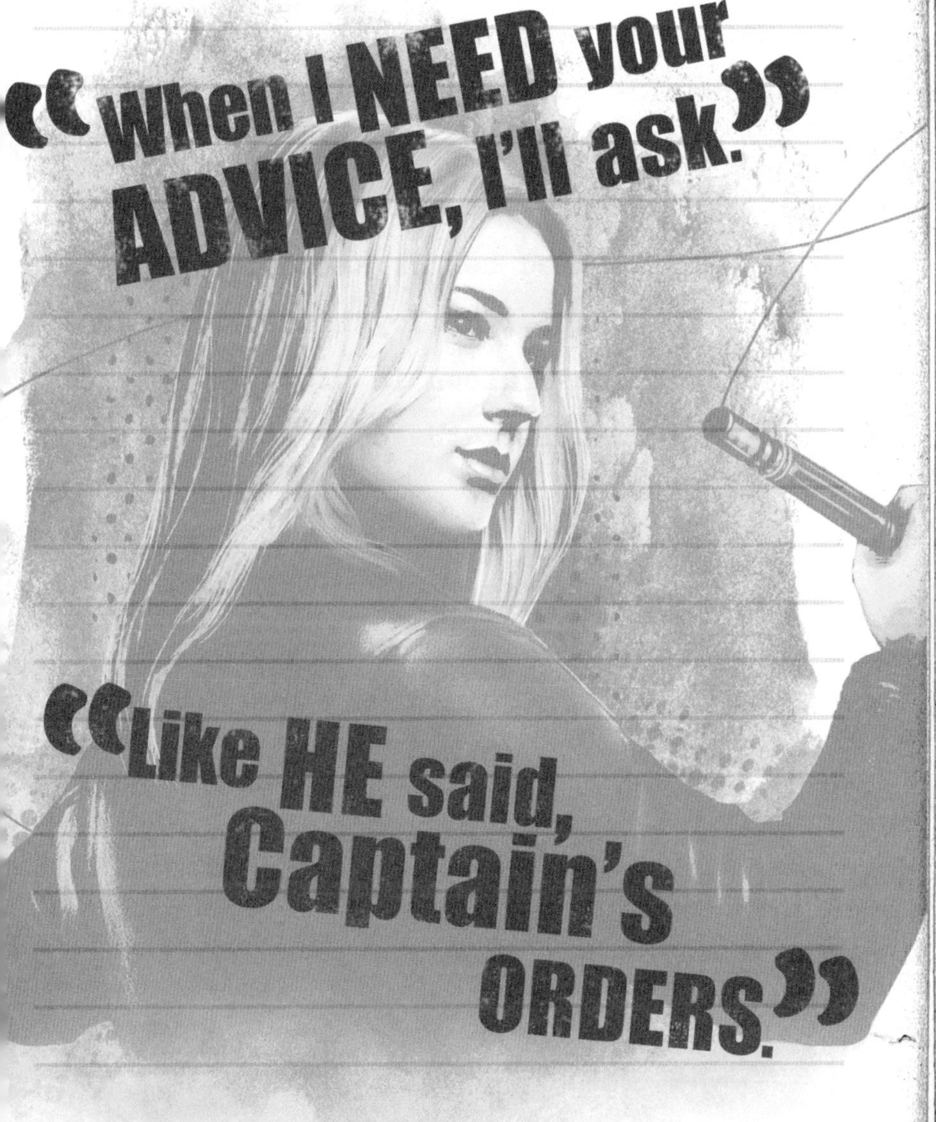
"When I NEED your ADVICE, I'll ask."
"Like HE said, Captain's ORDERS."

AGENT 13
HISTORY

Sharon Carter currently works in a special security detail, but was instrumental in the fall of S.H.I.E.L.D. after acting as one of their top agents for years. Once it was clear that Hydra had infiltrated her organization, Agent 13 was one of the handful of loyalists who aided Captain America and Falcon in stopping Project Insight and dismantling the corrupt S.H.I.E.L.D.

Friday,

Sharon worked closely with top agents.

the 2<del>0</del>1 02 <del>season</del>. a<del>g</del>ed <del>t</del>o <del>t</del>e side in

ed

l are
't
eir

she

that
es to

A
m
aga
H
Lyl
in
lin

Friday,

Agent 13 provides
expert tactical
assistance, planning
precise advanced
maneuvers.

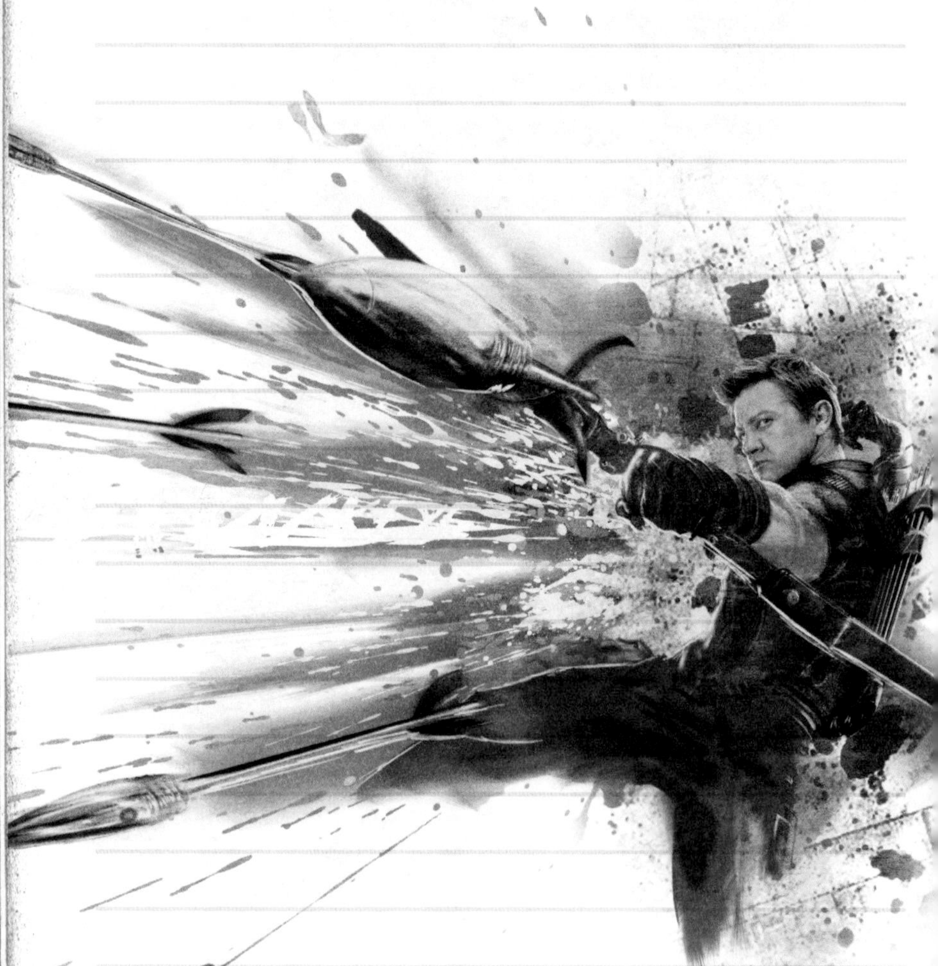

HAWKEYE

Clint Barton, a.k.a. Hawkeye, is a master archer and former agent of S.H.I.E.L.D. who joined the Avengers alongside his longtime partner, Black Widow. He uses his unparalleled mastery of the bow, along with a quiver of trick arrows, to make his point in any battle. Note: Even on a team like the Avengers, do NOT underestimate Hawkeye.

CONFIDENTIAL

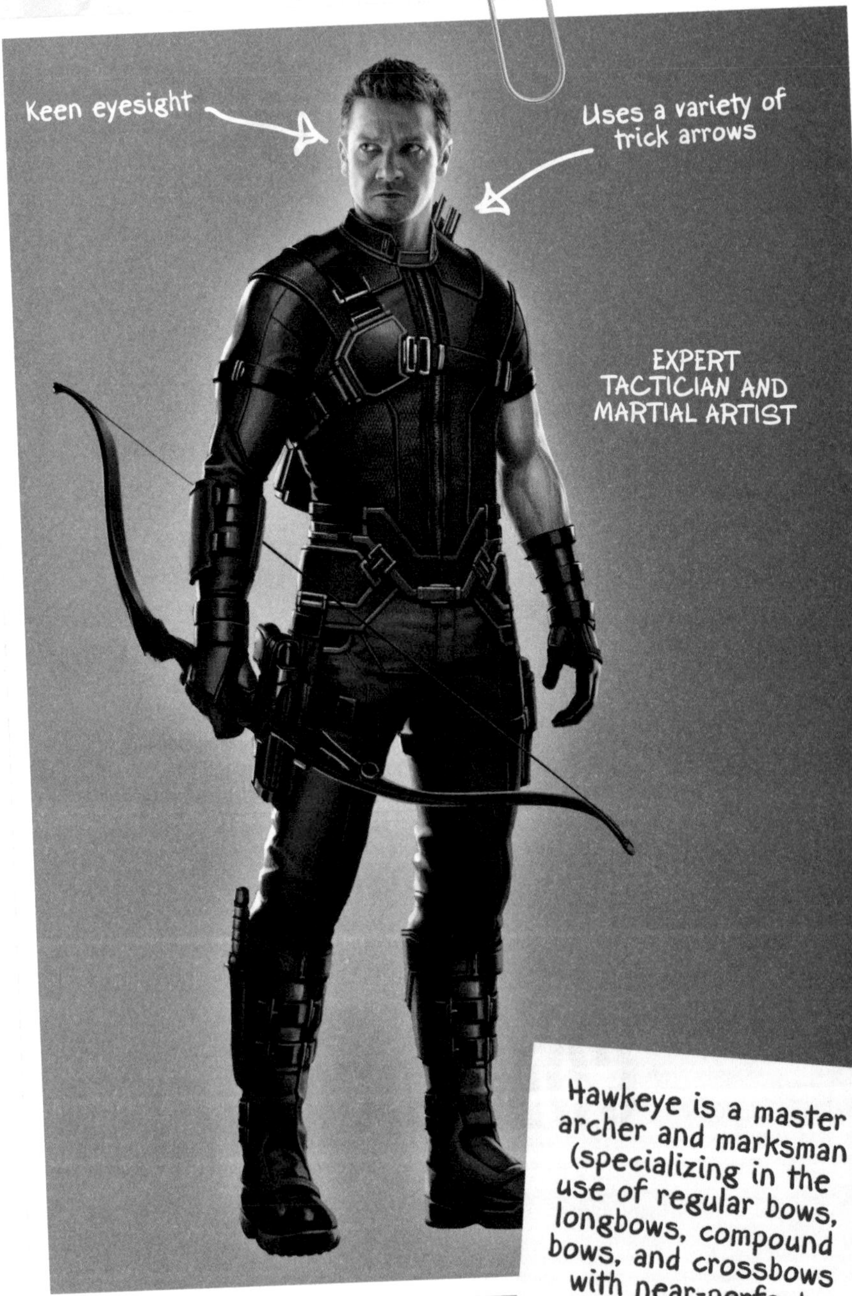
Keen eyesight
Uses a variety of trick arrows
EXPERT TACTICIAN AND MARTIAL ARTIST

Hawkeye is a master archer and marksman (specializing in the use of regular bows, longbows, compound bows, and crossbows with near-perfect accuracy).

HAWKEYE'S FAVORITE PHRASES

"I SEE better from a DISTANCE."

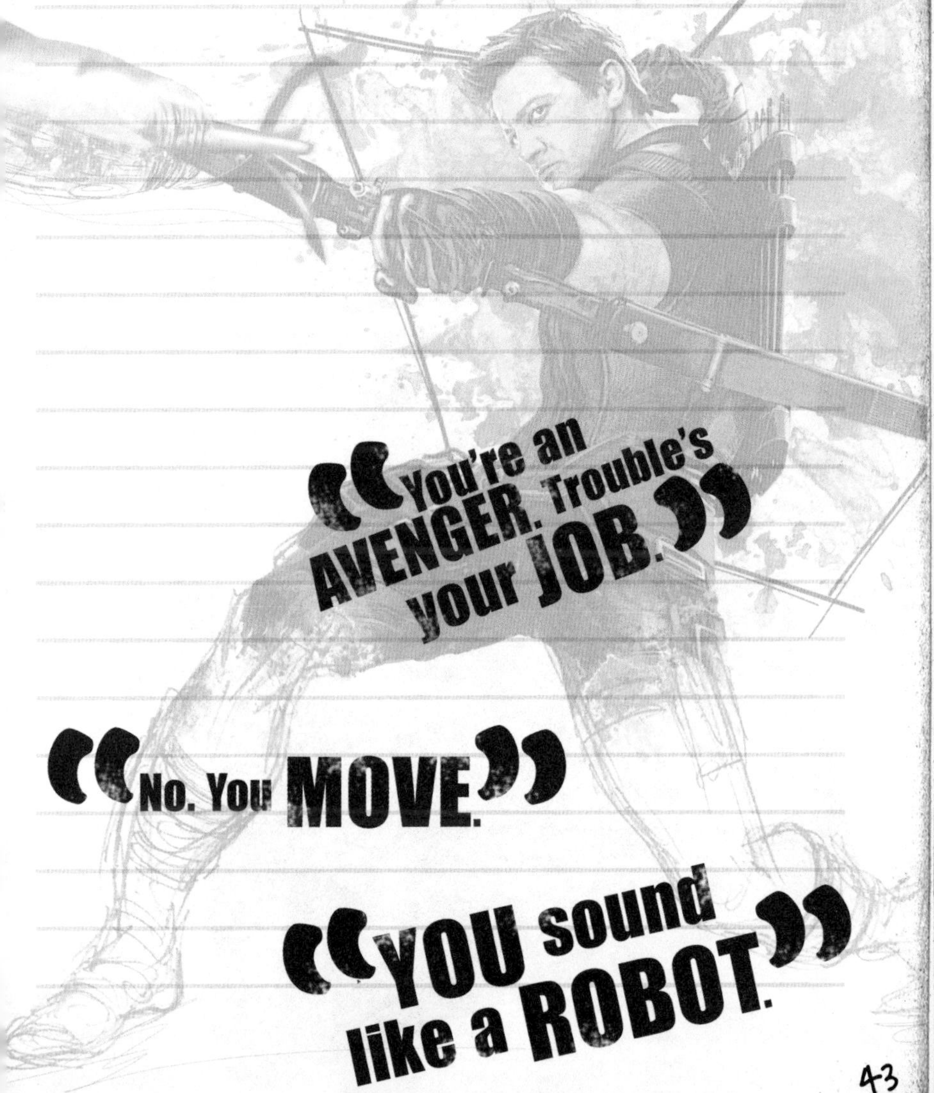

"You're an AVENGER. Trouble's your JOB."

"No. You MOVE."

"YOU sound like a ROBOT."

HAWKEYE
HISTORY

After Nick Fury asked Hawkeye to watch over
the Tesseract, he was brainwashed by the
Asgardian villain known as Loki. He helped Loki
destroy Project PEGASUS, but after the attacks
on the Hellicarrier, Clint was freed from Loki's
mind control by Black Widow and took his place
among the mighty Avengers. He then took
revenge against Loki and his army of Chitauri
soldiers in the Battle of New York.

Hawkeye uses a huge
variety of trick arrows to
gain the upper hand.

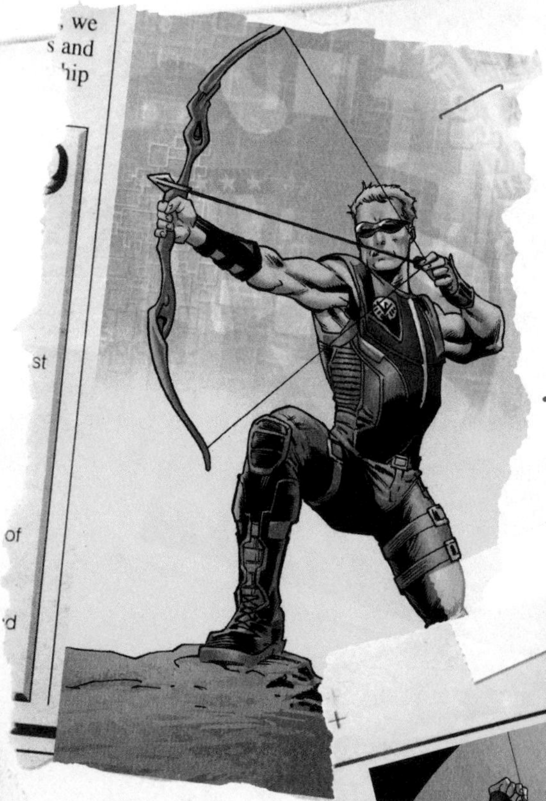

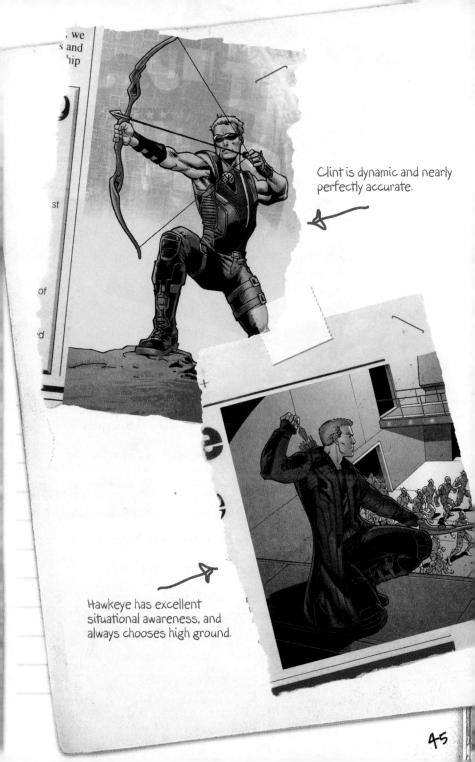

Clint is dynamic and nearly perfectly accurate.

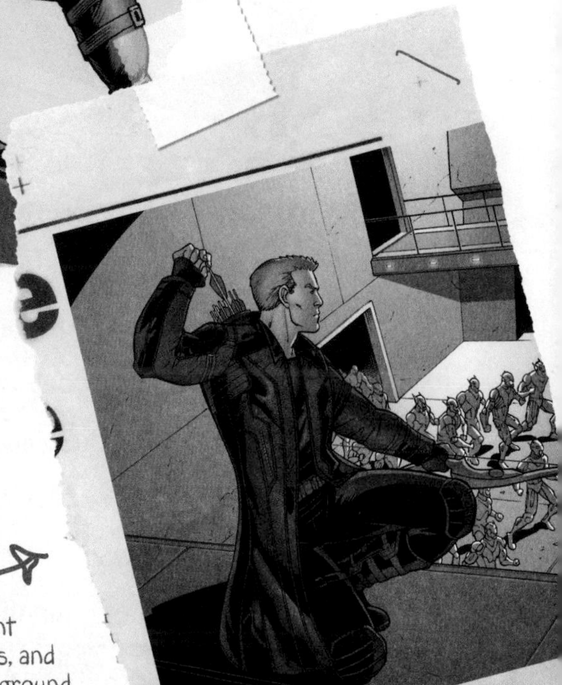

Hawkeye has excellent situational awareness, and always chooses high ground.

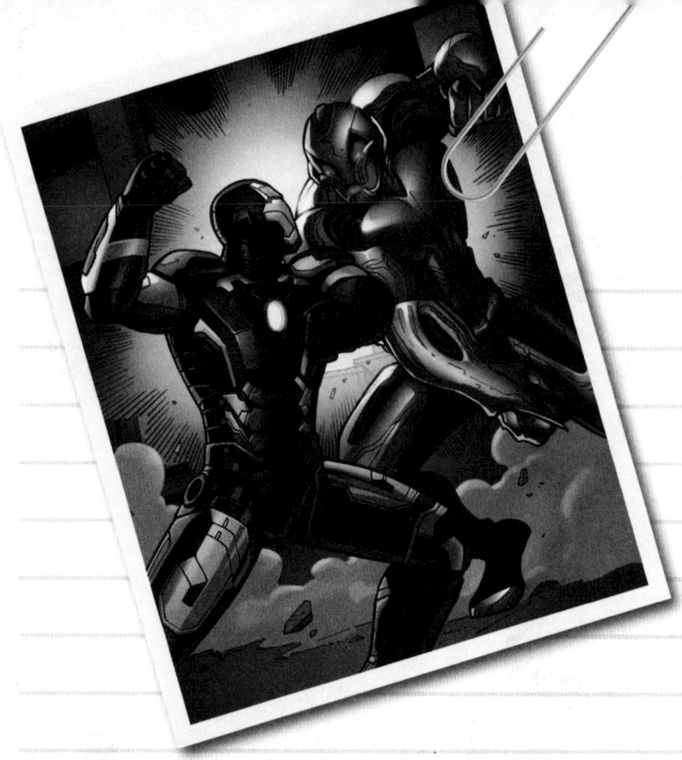

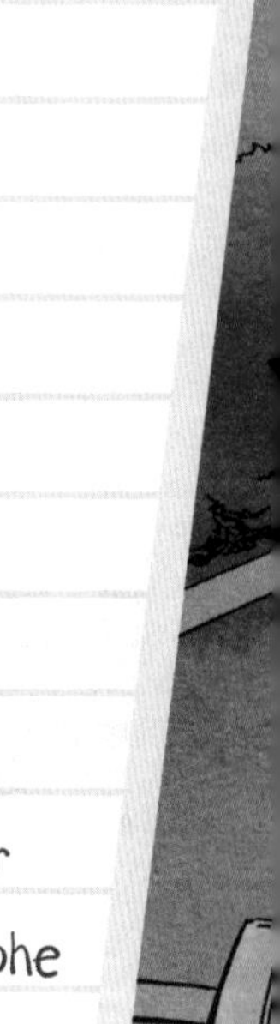

Having footed the bill for the Avengers' new facilities, Tony Stark was happy to set aside his Iron Man armor for a while. In the wake of Ultron's attack—a catastrophe for which he holds himself accountable—Tony now wants to focus on fostering the development of technologies that will benefit mankind. An opportunity for Tony to take responsibility arose when a collective world authority drafted the formerly mentioned Sokovia Accords, introducing accountability into the Avengers' operations.

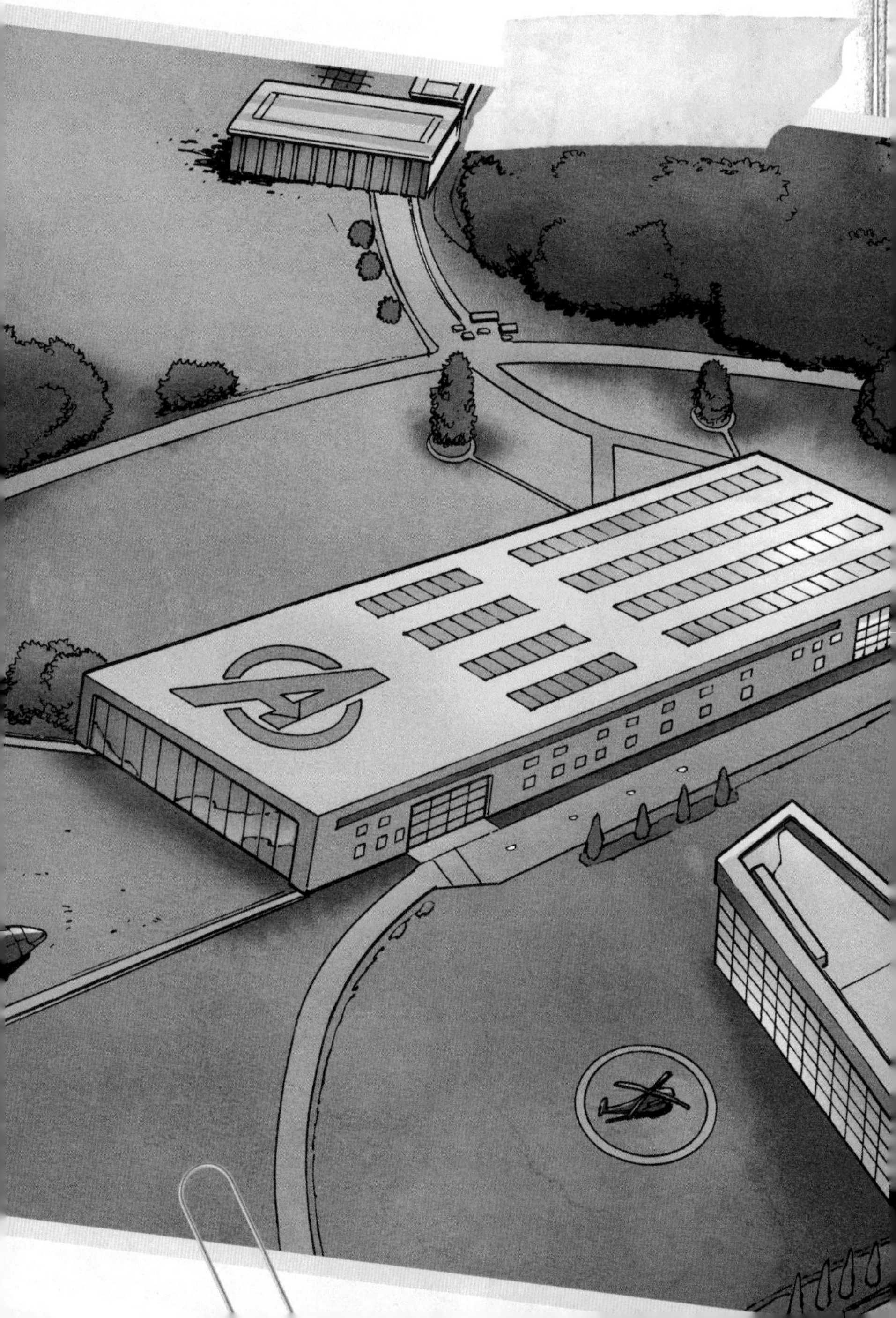

TEAM STARK

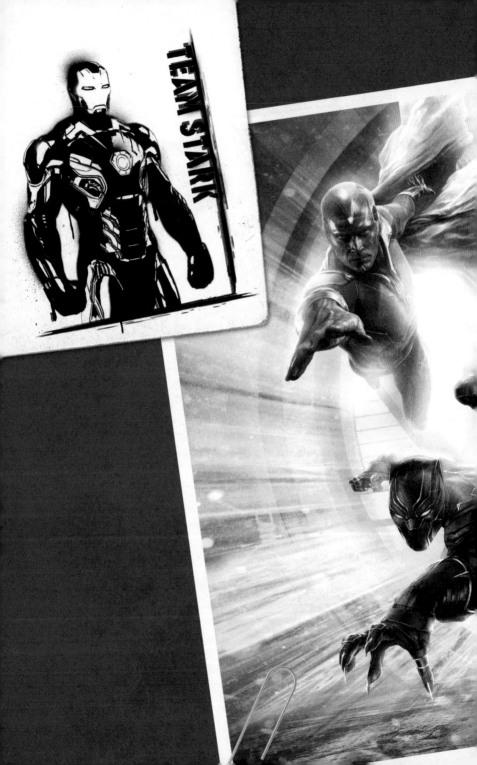

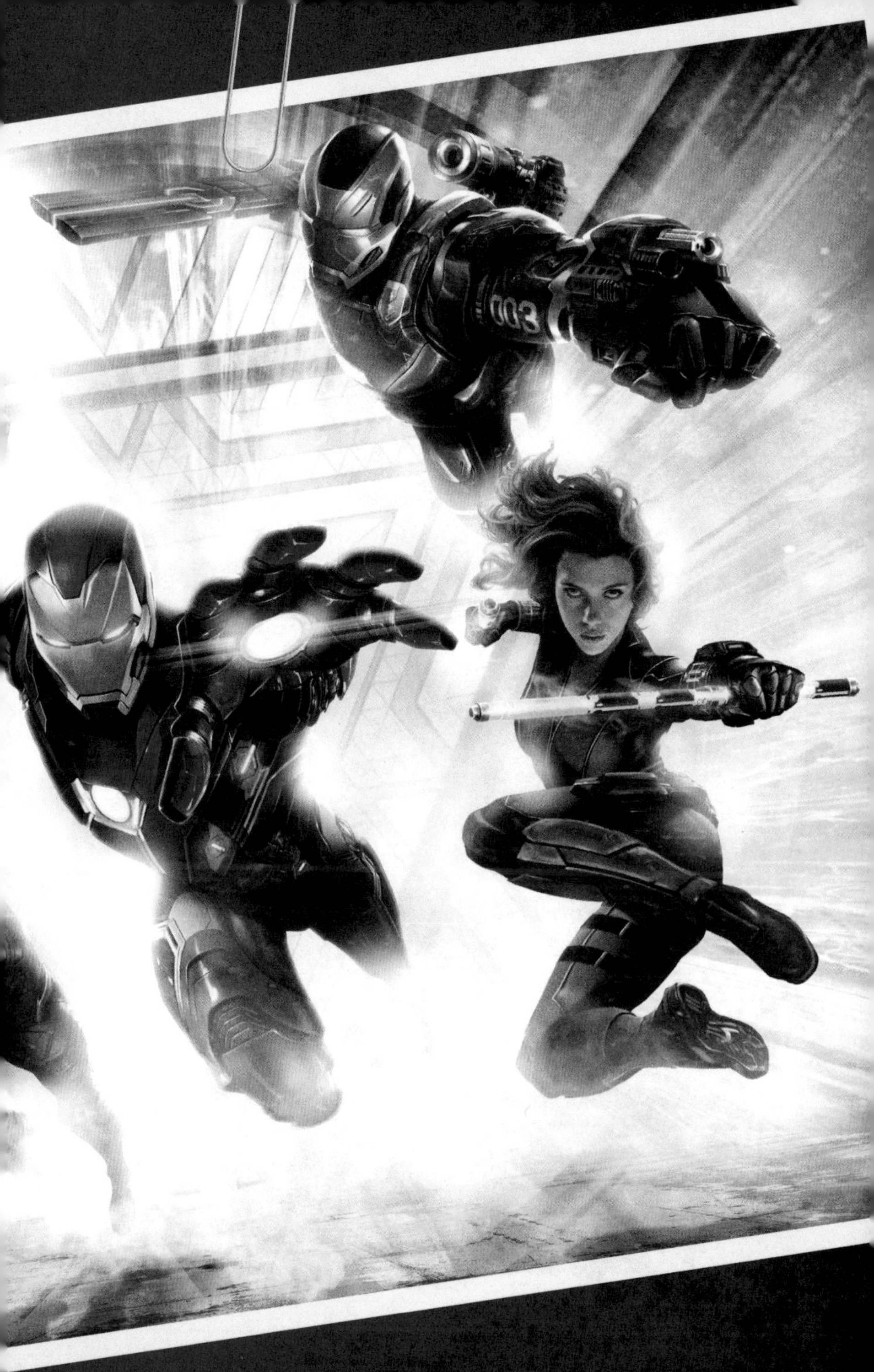
003

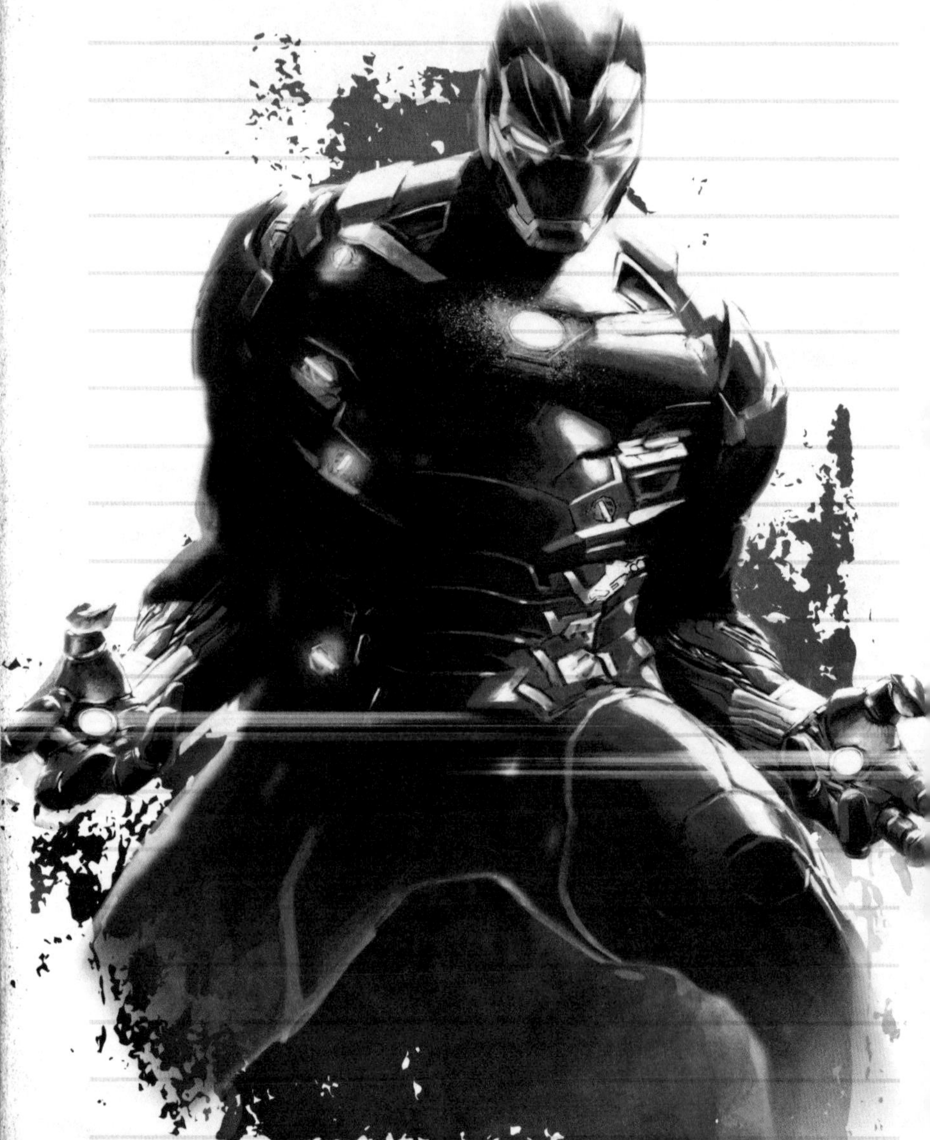

IRON MAN

Ever since an incident overseas inspired him to create an invincible suit of armor, the eccentric inventor and billionaire Tony Stark has dedicated his life to using his advanced technology to protect the world. The chief source of funding and equipment for the Avengers, Stark still finds time to suit up and join Earth's Mightiest Heroes as Iron Man.

CONFIDENTIAL

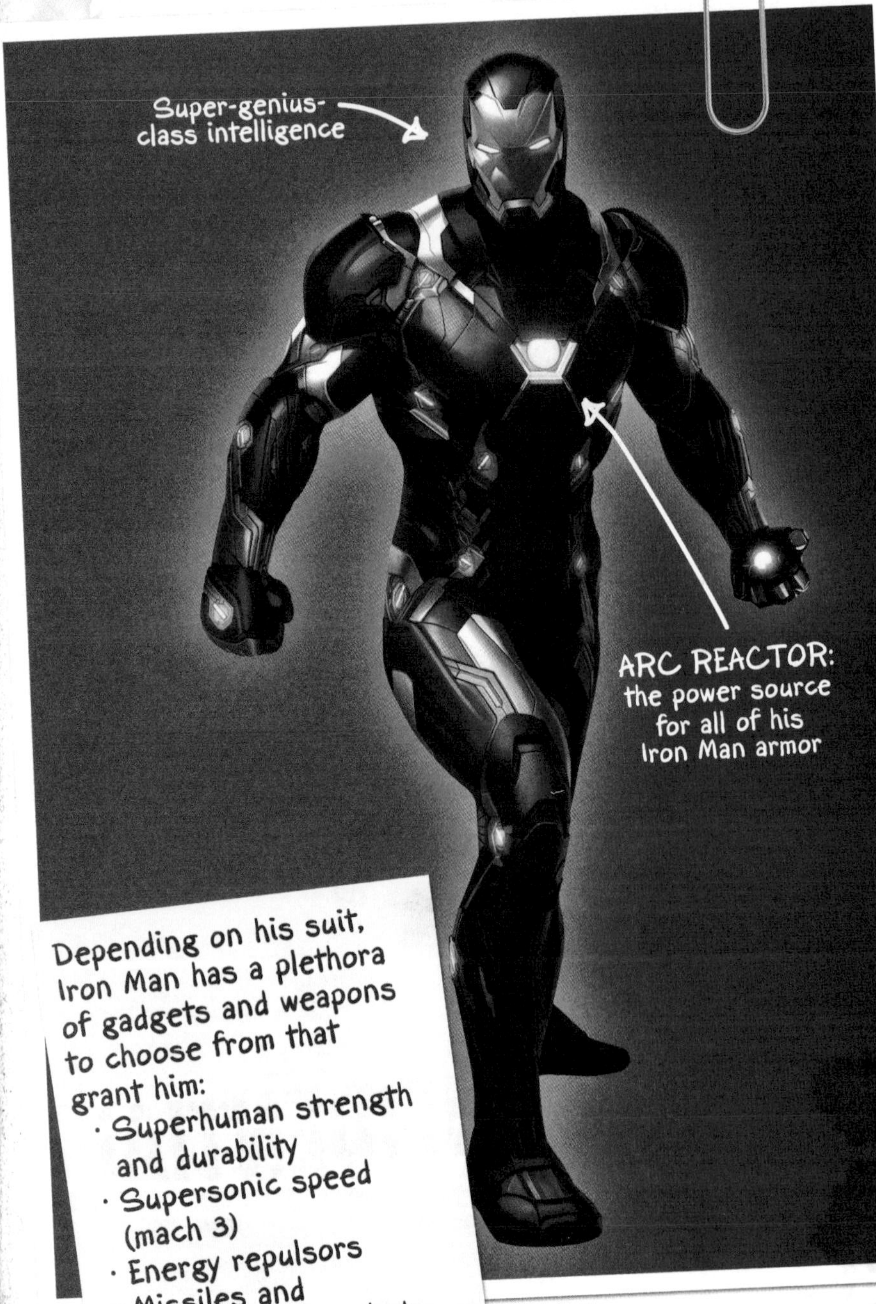
Super-genius-class intelligence
ARC REACTOR: the power source for all of his Iron Man armor

Depending on his suit, Iron Man has a plethora of gadgets and weapons to choose from that grant him:

- Superhuman strength and durability
- Supersonic speed (mach 3)
- Energy repulsors
- Missiles and heat-seeking rockets

IRON MAN'S FAVORITE PHRASES

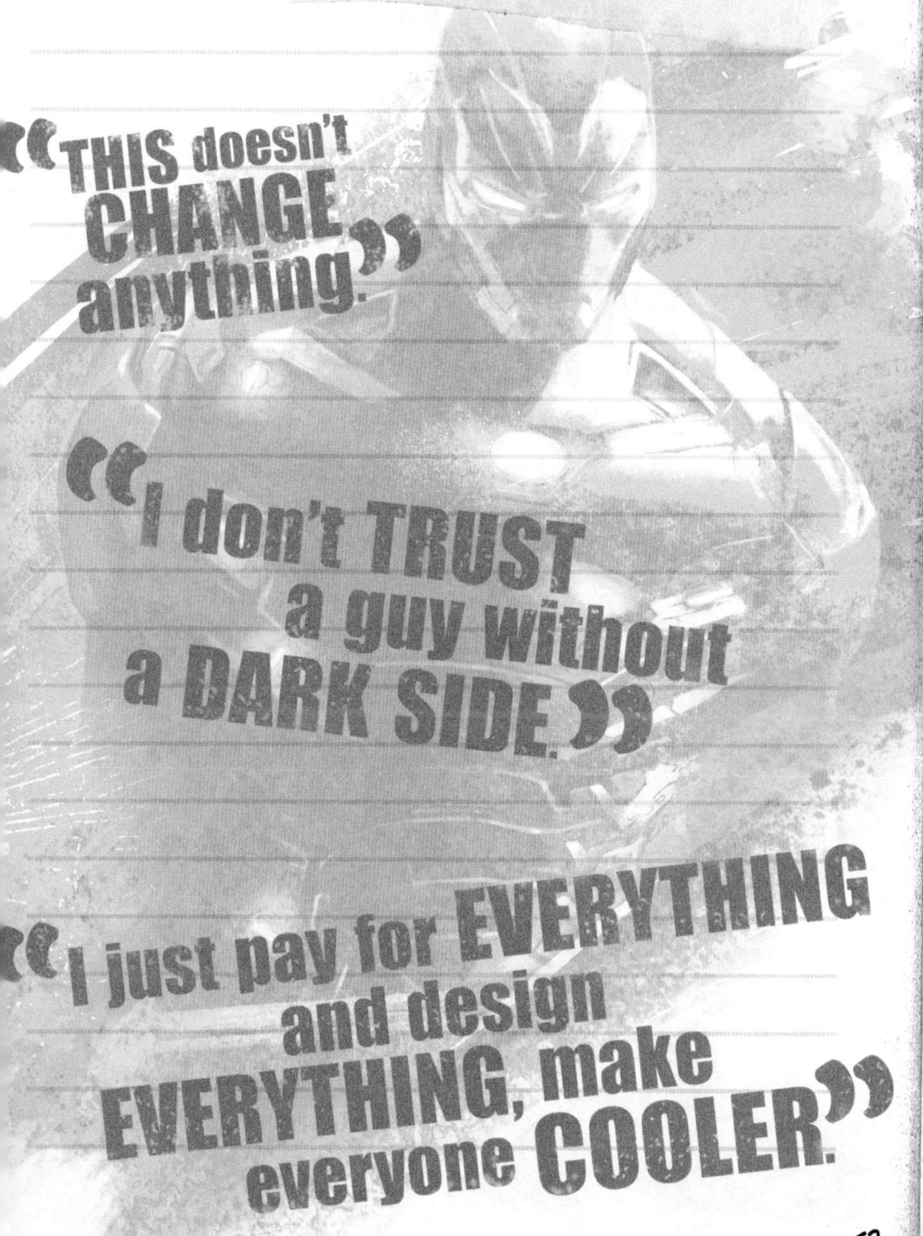

"THIS doesn't CHANGE anything."

"I don't TRUST a guy without a DARK SIDE."

"I just pay for EVERYTHING and design EVERYTHING, make everyone COOLER."

IRON MAN HISTORY

Tony Stark suffered post-traumatic stress disorder due to the Battle of New York, in which he barely defeated Loki and his Chitauri army. To relieve this stress, Tony Stark created the Iron Legion: a group of robots that patrolled the world seeking peace and stopping those who promote death and destruction.

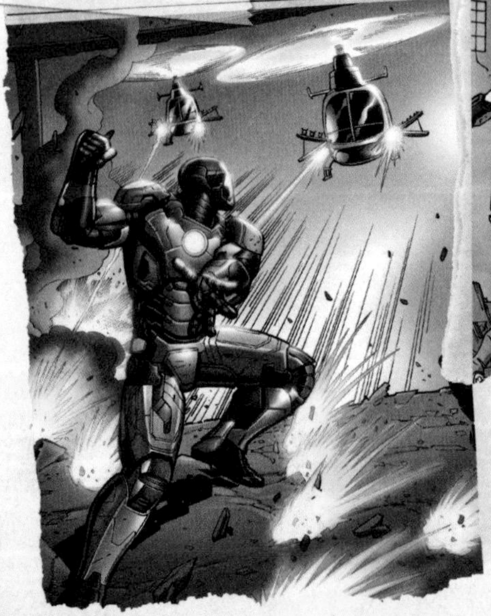

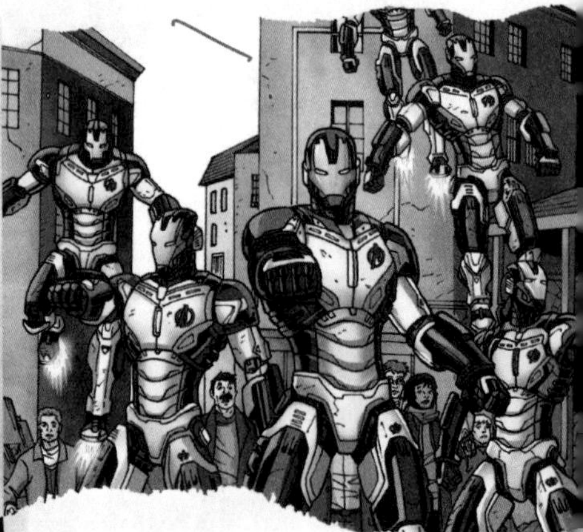

Tony, with the help of Bruce Banner, built the
Ultron program in hopes that it would act as
a peacekeeping AI, or artificial intelligence.
Tony wanted to create an Iron Man suit that
the planet could wear: Once an incoming threat
from space was detected and neared Earth,
Ultron would react, protecting Earth from
harm. But the program rebelled and chose to
destroy all of humanity instead. The Avengers
defeted Ultron but at a cost. The old team
disassembled and Tony Stark retired. Until
now...

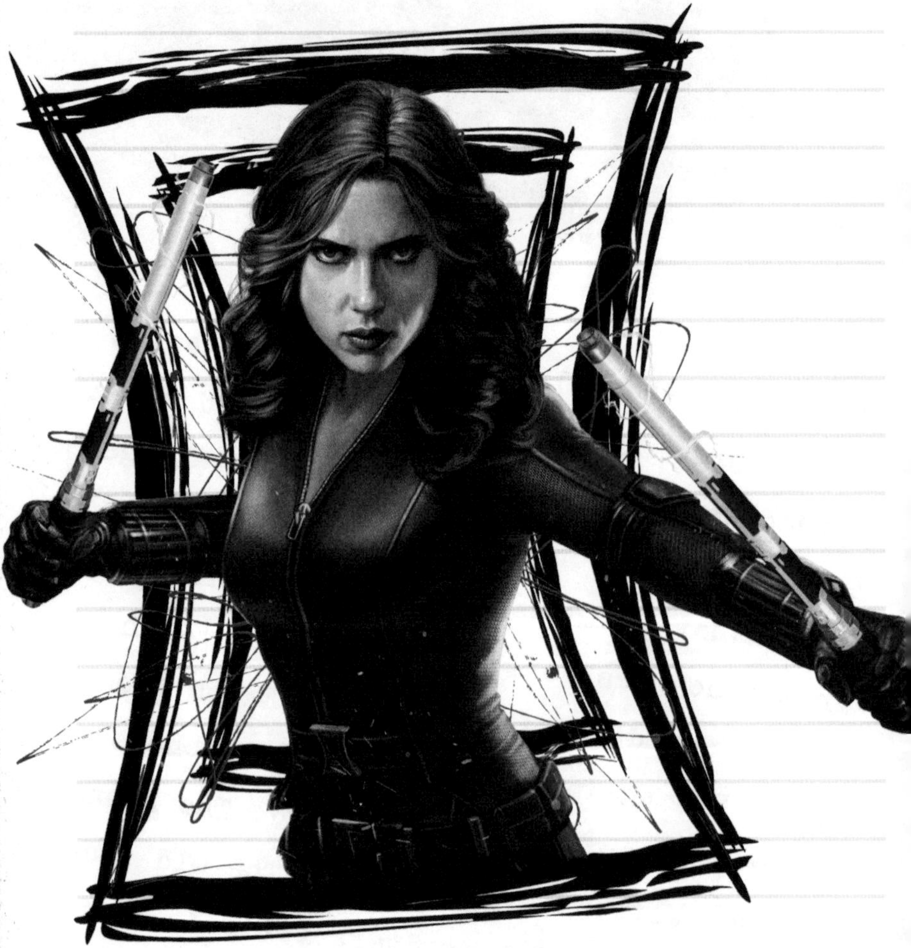

BLACK WIDOW

Originally one of the most dangerous and prolific S.H.I.E.L.D. agents, Natasha Romanoff, a.k.a. Black Widow, has found her true family alongside her fellow Avengers. Though Romanoff's dark past still haunts her, she now uses her formidable skills, developed by a shadowy organization through forced training, to defend the innocent.

CONFIDENTIAL

57

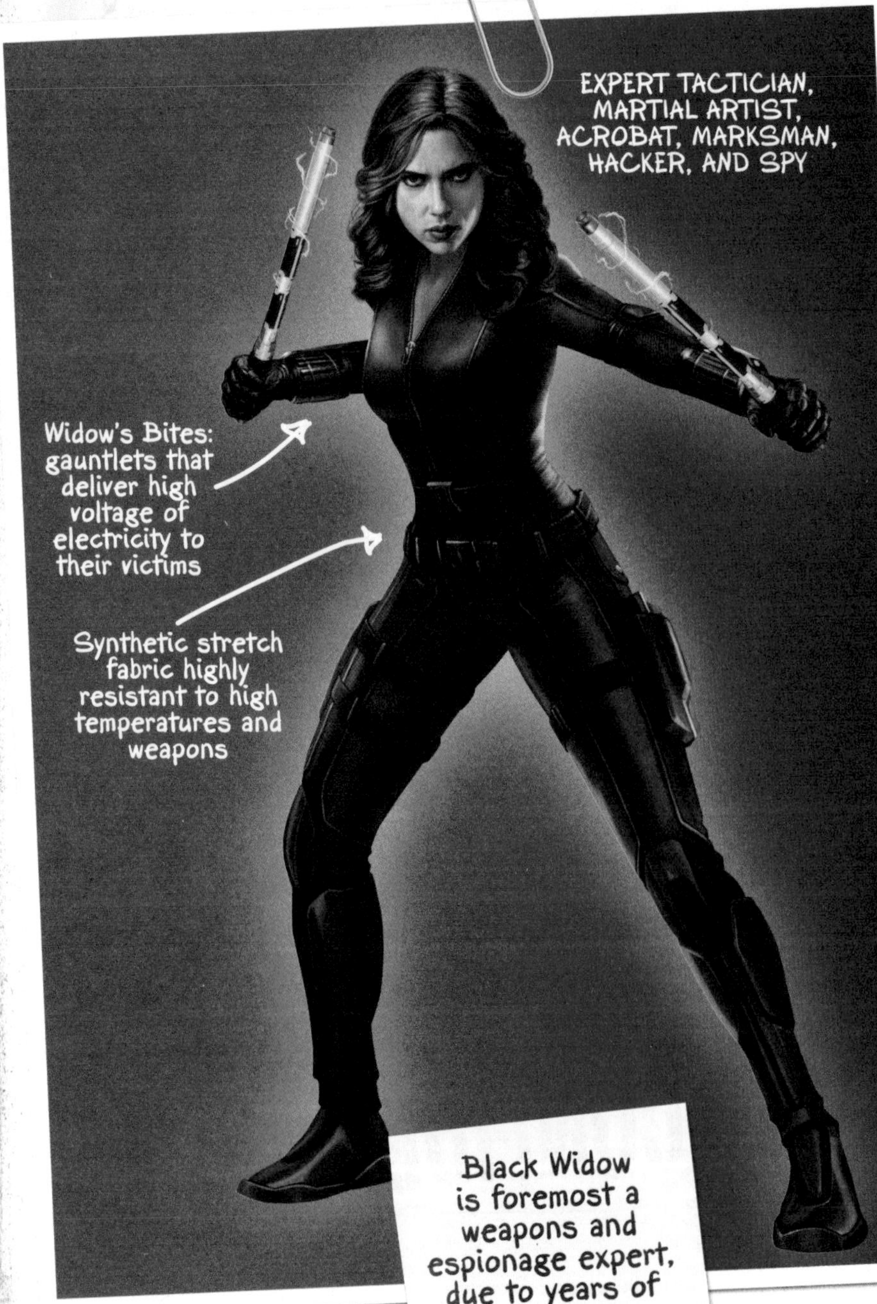
EXPERT TACTICIAN, MARTIAL ARTIST, ACROBAT, MARKSMAN, HACKER, AND SPY
Widow's Bites: gauntlets that deliver high voltage of electricity to their victims
Synthetic stretch fabric highly resistant to high temperatures and weapons

Black Widow is foremost a weapons and espionage expert, due to years of brutal training.

BLACK WIDOW'S FAVORITE PHRASES

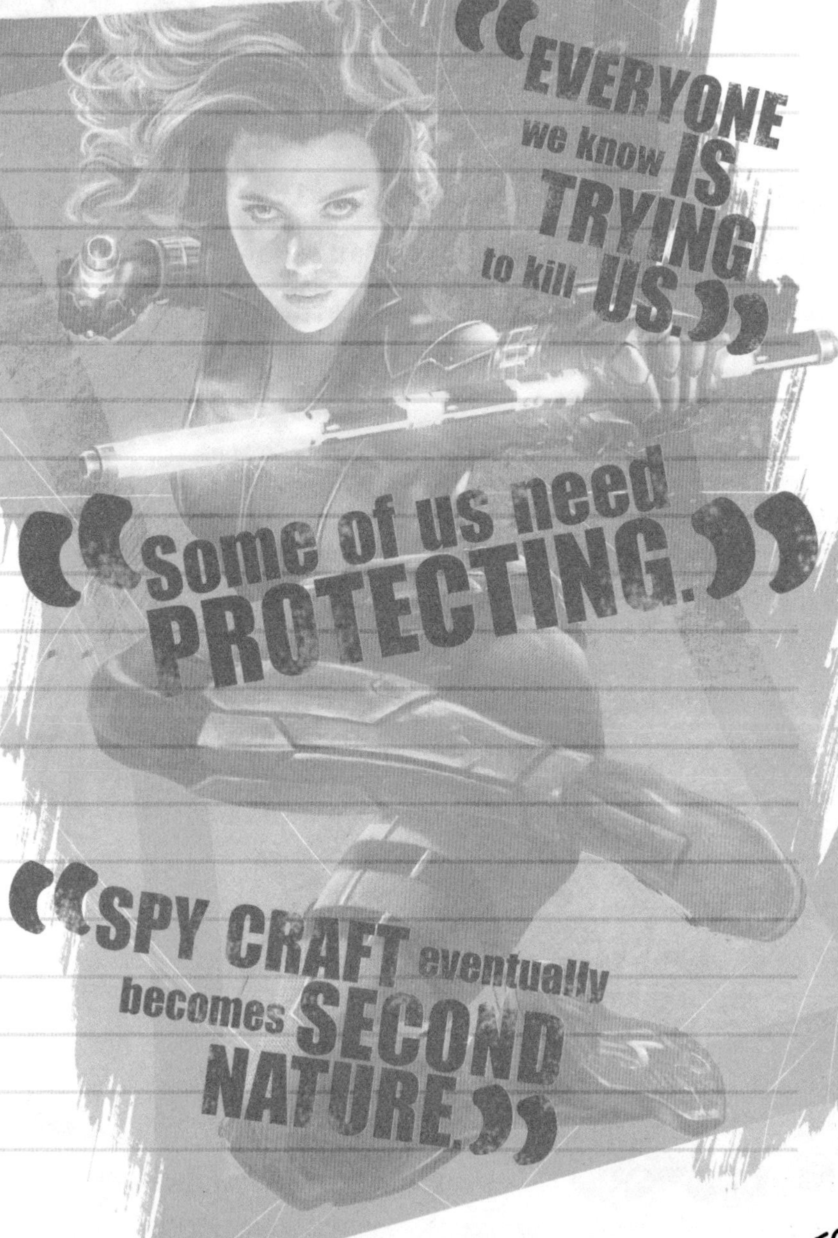

"EVERYONE we know IS TRYING to kill US."

"Some of us need PROTECTING."

"SPY CRAFT eventually becomes SECOND NATURE."

BLACK WIDOW HISTORY

When Loki declared war on Earth, Black Widow joined the Avengers. Armed with her Widow's Bites, Natasha helped defend New York City and defeat Loki and the Chitauri.

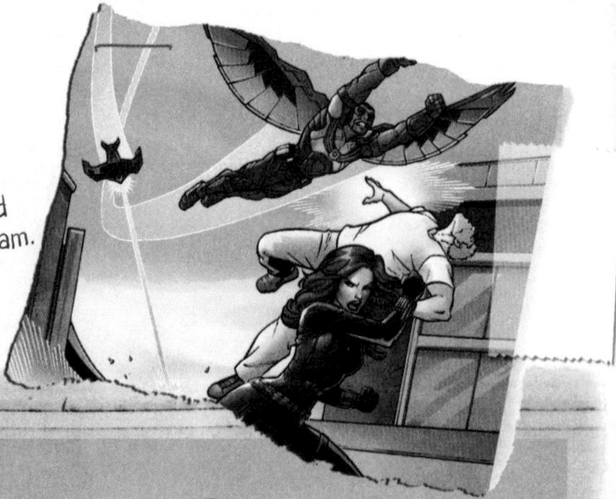

Black Widow is a skilled fighter—solo or in a team.

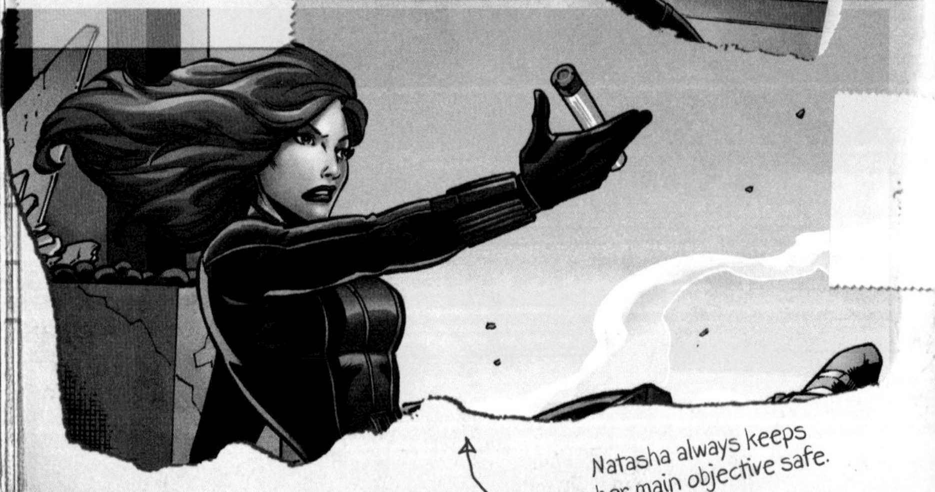

Natasha always keeps her main objective safe.

After the Avengers defeated Loki, Natasha continued to work with S.H.I.E.L.D., this time teaming up with fellow agent Captain America. When the Hydra uprising occurred, all of Natasha's dark past deeds were revealed to the world. She dropped

off the grid and began to rebuild her cover. Eventually, she rejoined the Avengers and worked to take down various Hydra bases across the world. She was also a key player in destroying Ultron. Unlike most of the original members of the Avengers, Black Widow remained a member of the second incarnation of the team after the war against Ultron.

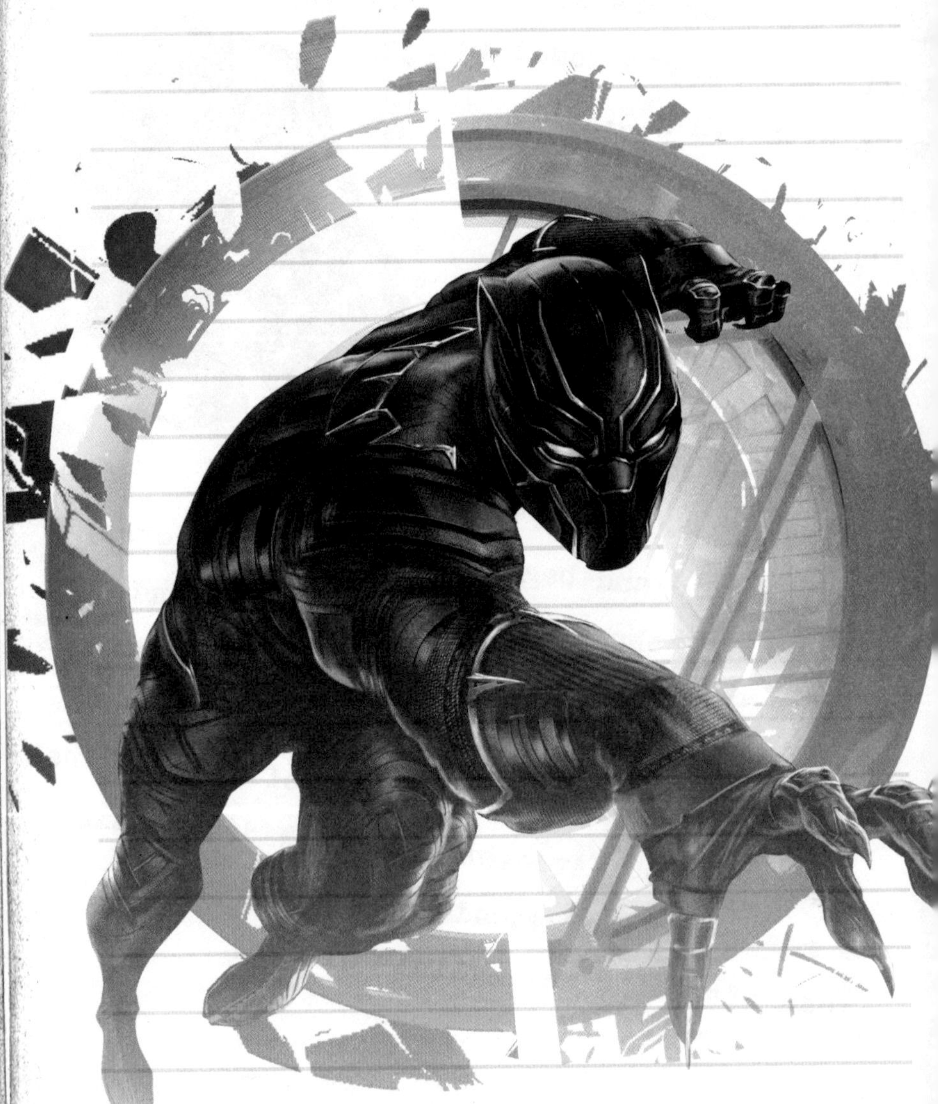

BLACK PANTHER

The prince of the technologically advanced but reclusive African nation Wakanda, Prince T'Challa's birthright is not only to rule, but to don the mantle of Black Panther, a powerful warrior and symbol to his people. T'Challa will aggressively defend his country and citizens against any threat, no matter how menacing.

CONFIDENTIAL

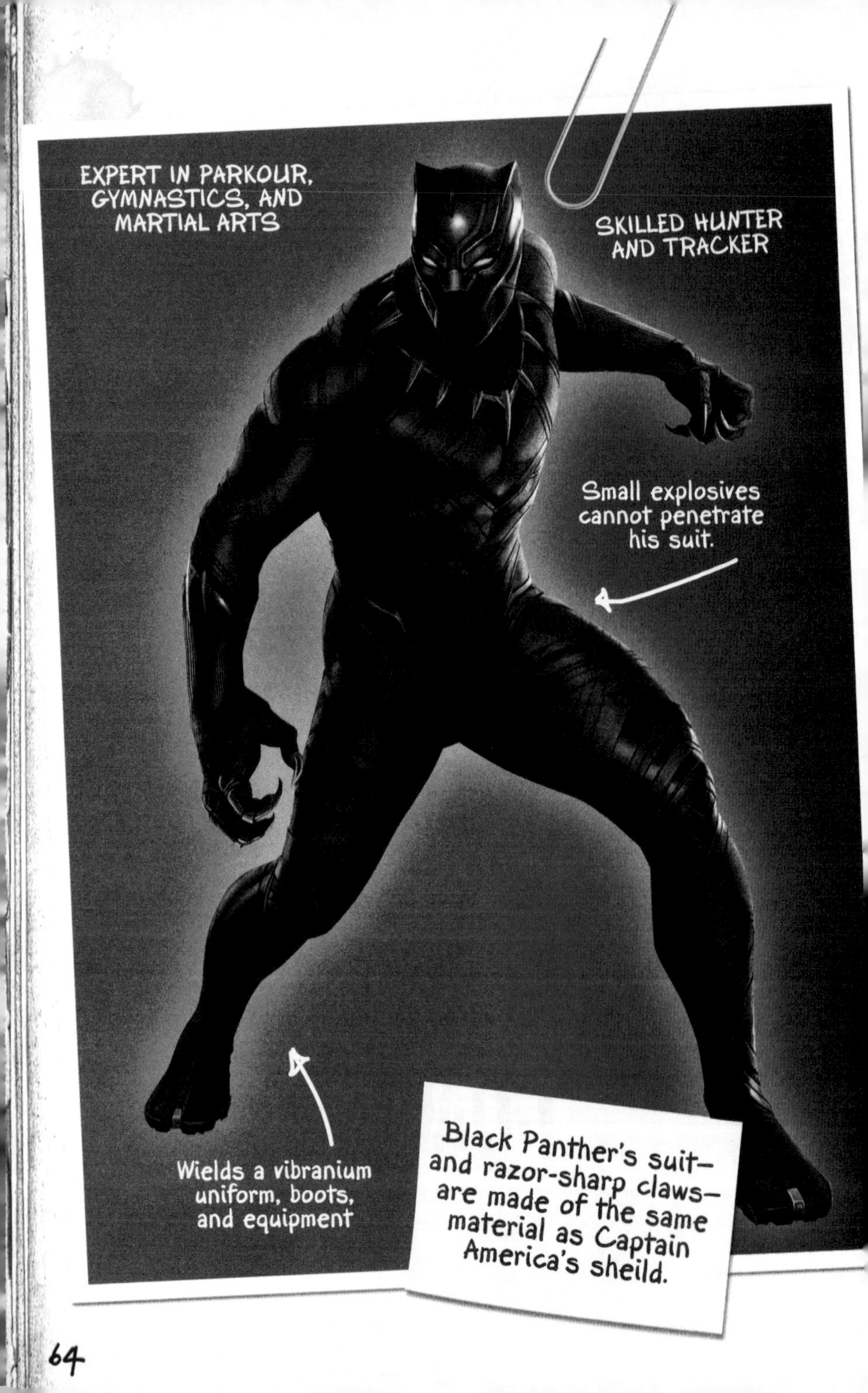
EXPERT IN PARKOUR, GYMNASTICS, AND MARTIAL ARTS
SKILLED HUNTER AND TRACKER
Small explosives cannot penetrate his suit.
Wields a vibranium uniform, boots, and equipment

Black Panther's suit—and razor-sharp claws—are made of the same material as Captain America's sheild.

BLACK PANTHER'S FAVORITE PHRASES

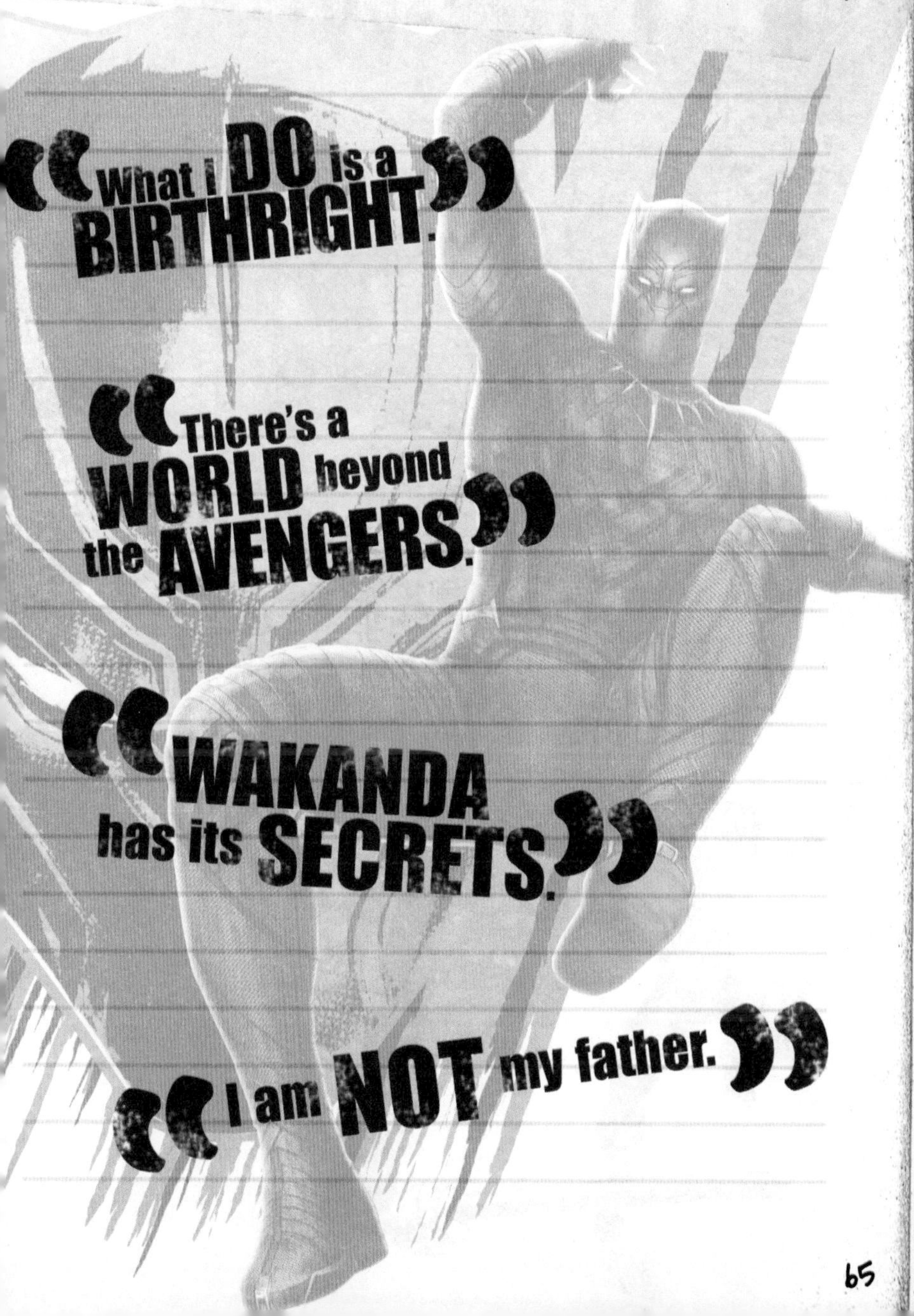

"What I DO is a BIRTHRIGHT."

"There's a WORLD beyond the AVENGERS."

"WAKANDA has its SECRETS."

"I am NOT my father."

BLACK PANTHER HISTORY

Black Panther is able to go toe-to-toe with the top fighters in the world.

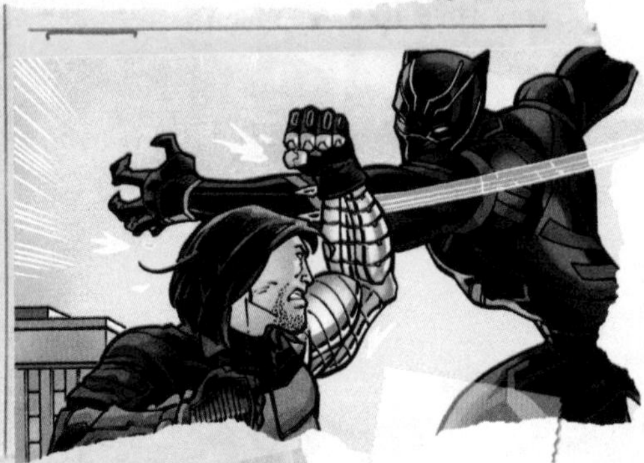

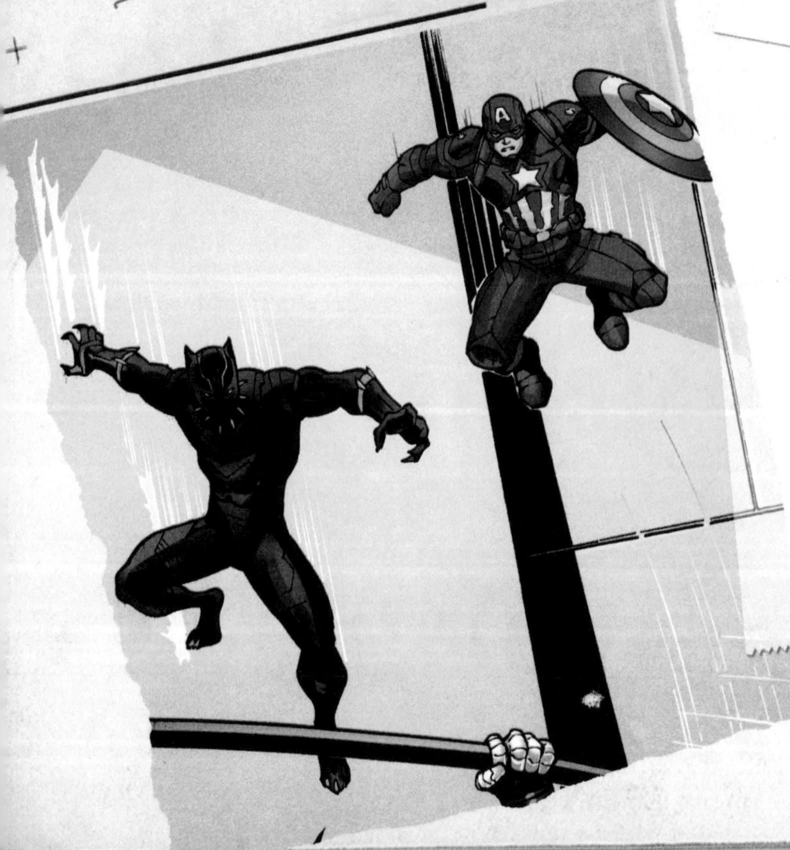

Black Panther's motivations remain unclear.

Not much is known about the history of the mysterious Black Panther. The royal bloodline of Wakanda has passed down the title and equipment from parent to child, each new hero entrusted with the protection of their home country. T'Challa is the newest prince to call himself Black Panther, and it appears he has designs on dealing with the Avengers.

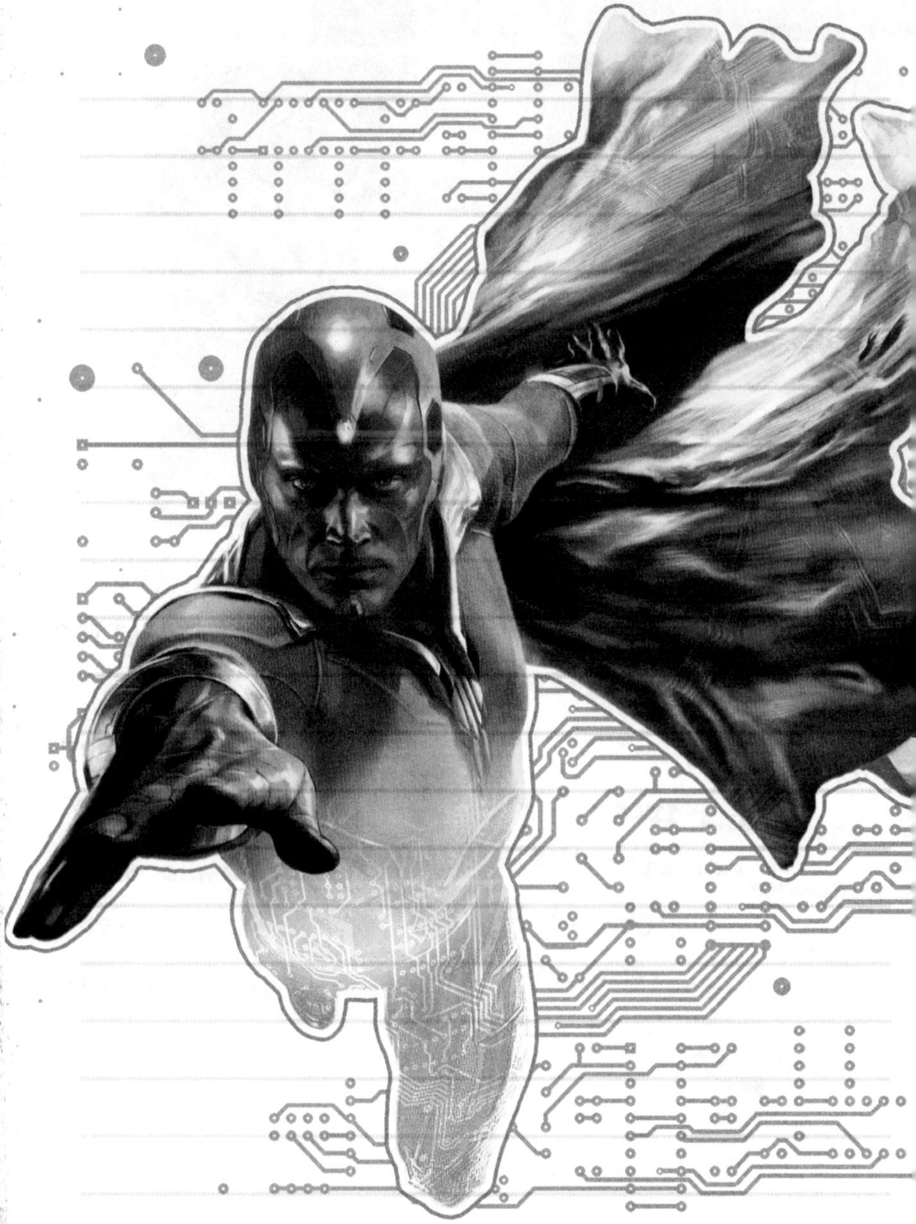

VISION

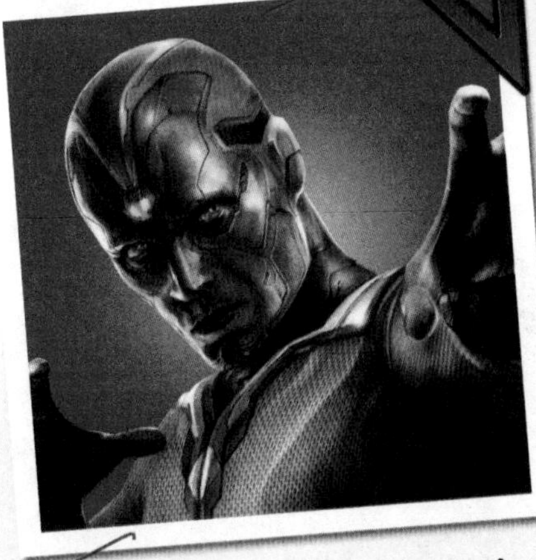

The Vision is a sentient artificial intelligence housed in a highly advanced synthetic body. Since joining the Avengers, Vision has endeavored to further understand humans and his place among them. Though he has yet to come to a definitive conclusion, Vision knows it is his responsibility to use his incredible powers to protect the world in which he now lives.

CONFIDENTIAL

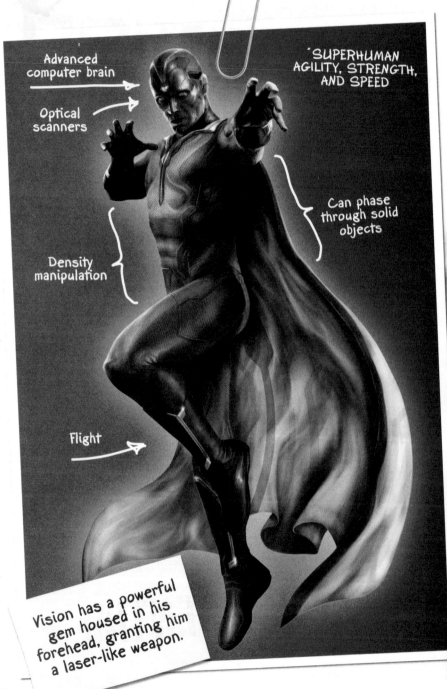

Advanced
computer brain

Optical
scanners

SUPERHUMAN
AGILITY, STRENGTH,
AND SPEED

Can phase
through solid
objects

Density
manipulation

Flight

Vision has a powerful gem housed in his forehead, granting him a laser-like weapon.

VISION'S FAVORITE PHRASES

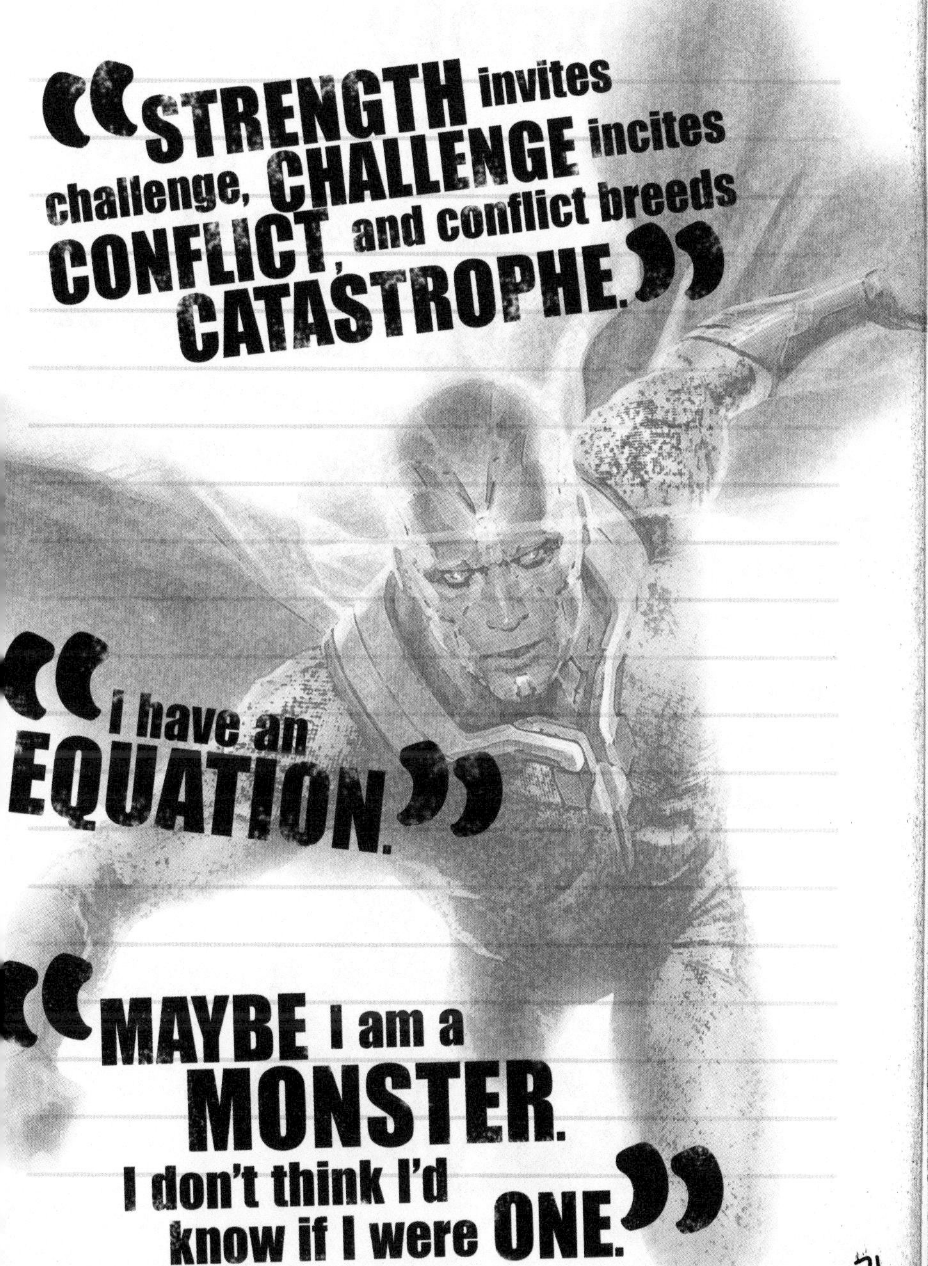

"STRENGTH invites challenge, CHALLENGE incites CONFLICT, and conflict breeds CATASTROPHE."

"I have an EQUATION."

"MAYBE I am a MONSTER. I don't think I'd know if I were ONE."

THE VISION
HISTORY

The Vision is a powerful synthetic being born from a vibranium-laced body created by Ultron and Helen Cho, programmed by Tony Stark and Bruce Banner using JARVIS-based codes, and activated by the mind stone hidden inside Loki's scepter. He was given a benevolent personality and a fondness for humans, the opposite of Ultron. He joined the Avengers and led the charge to stopping Ultron and his war against humanity. The Vision officially became a member of the second Avengers team, led by Captain America.

in
the
as a
sation
g was

ket to
, and

would

Vision has become a stabalizing force for the Avengers.

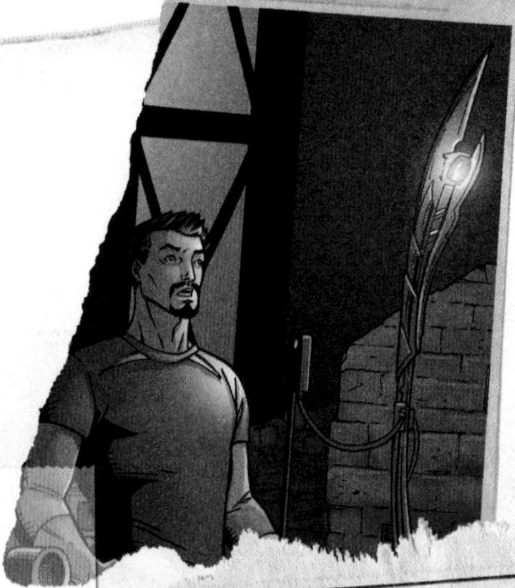

Vision was created when Tony Stark used the "remains" of JARVIS to form a new AI, given life by the gem in Loki's scepter.

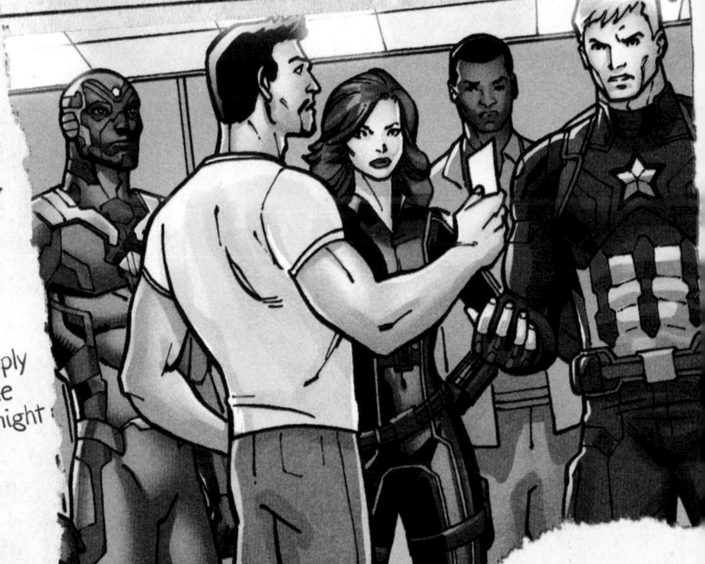

Attempting to apply strict logic to the latest conflict might prove difficult.

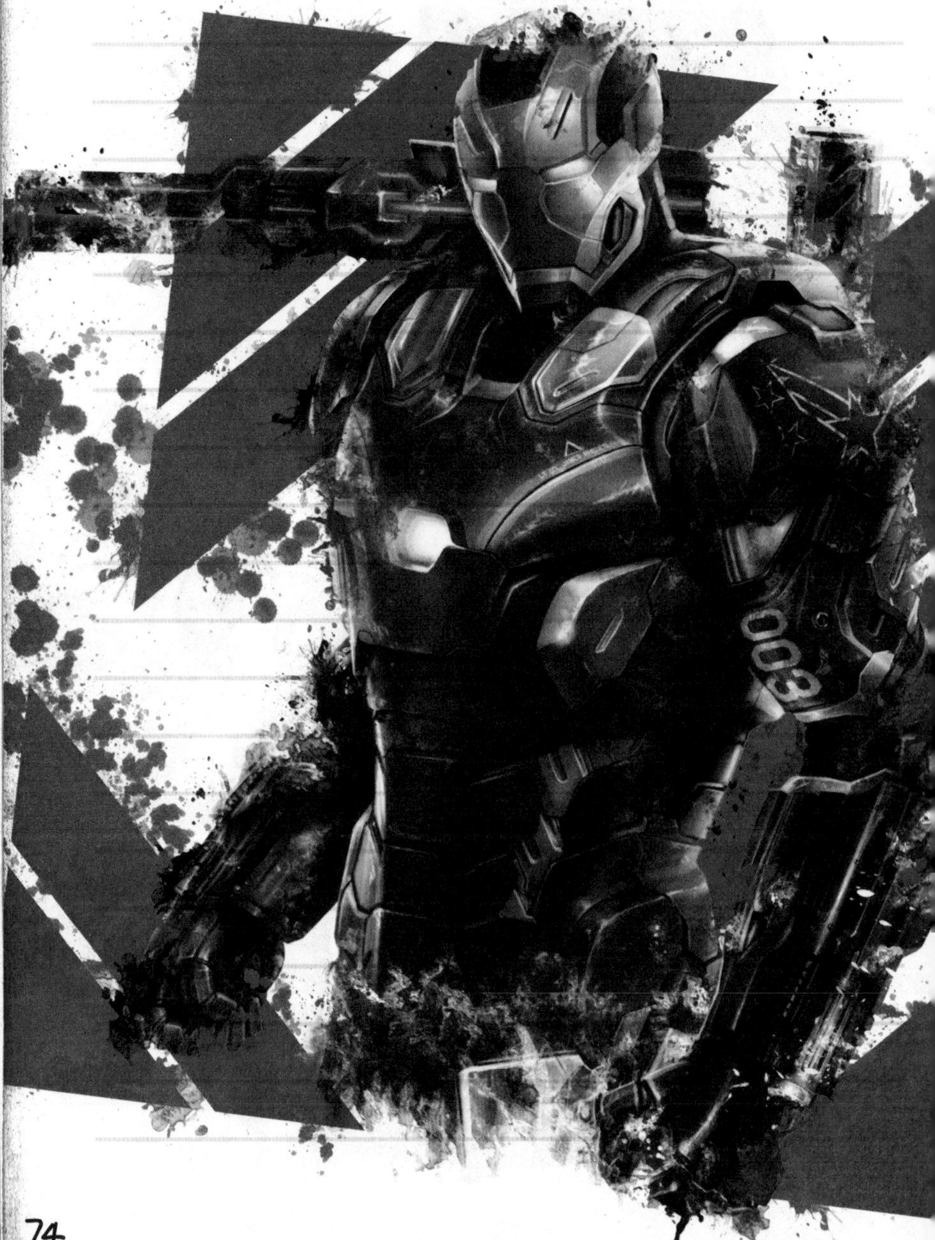
003

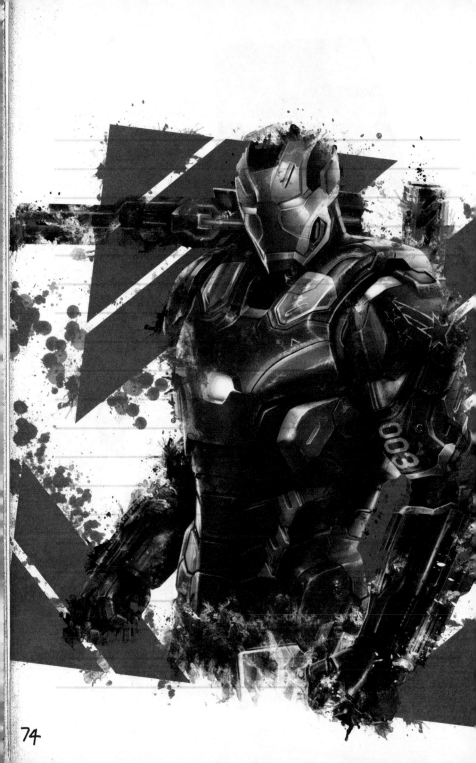

WAR MACHINE

Colonel James "Rhodey" Rhodes has long served as both Tony Stark's best friend and the government's special liaison to Stark Industries. In battle, Rhodey dons the War Machine armor, a modified variant of Tony's own Iron Man suit. Armed with a new modular Gatling cannon and enough firepower to take on a legion of enemies, War Machine is a true one-man army.

CONFIDENTIAL

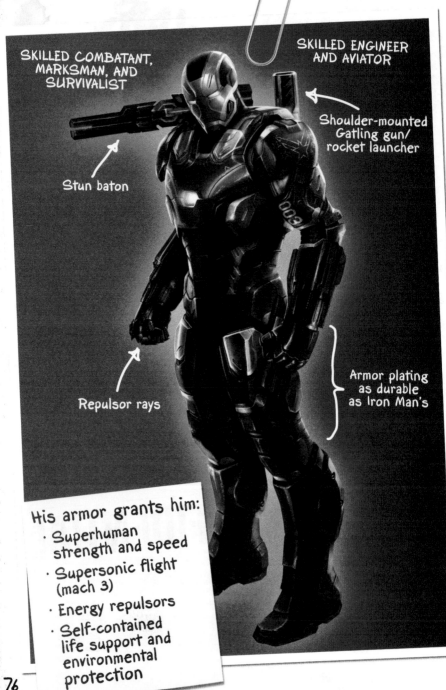

SKILLED COMBATANT, MARKSMAN, AND SURVIVALIST

SKILLED ENGINEER AND AVIATOR

Shoulder-mounted Gatling gun/ rocket launcher

Stun baton

Repulsor rays

Armor plating as durable as Iron Man's

His armor grants him:
- Superhuman strength and speed
- Supersonic flight (mach 3)
- Energy repulsors
- Self-contained life support and environmental protection

WAR MACHINE'S FAVORITE PHRASES

"War Machine COMIN' right ATCHA!"

"UNLIMITED force authorized!"

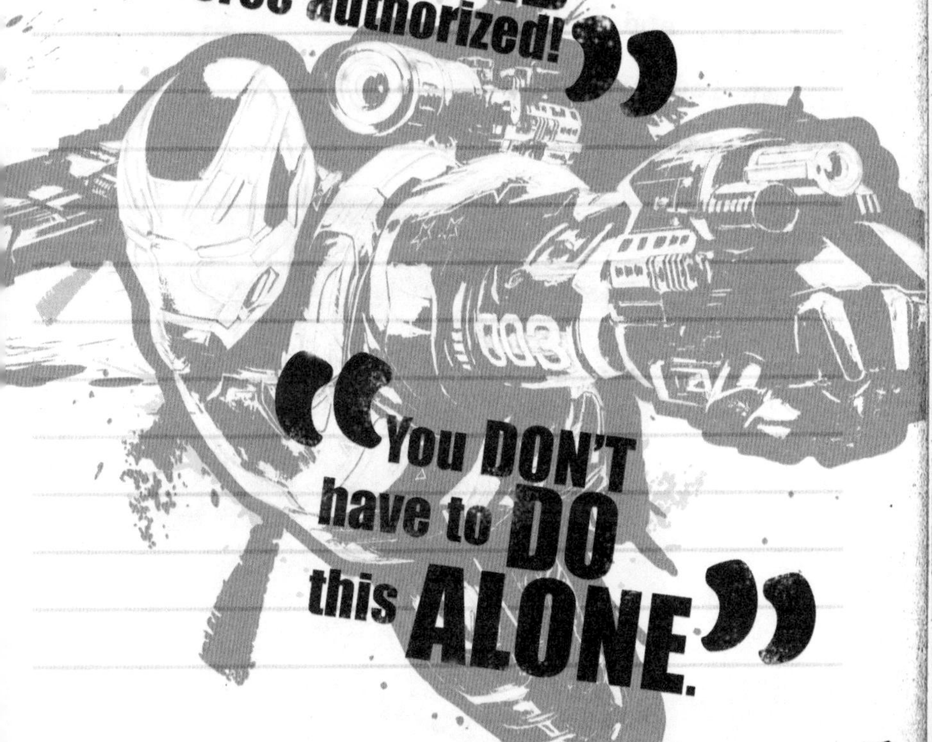

"You DON'T have to DO this ALONE."

WAR MACHINE'S
HISTORY

After proving his worth during the battle
of Sokovia, in which he battled an army
of Ultron's sentries, War Machine was seen as
a key asset in preventing another attack in
the future. With the war against Ultron
finished, Rhodey, along with Vision, Wanda
Maximoff, and Falcon, joined the new Avengers
roster led by Captain America and Black Widow
on a more permanent basis.

War Machine's
flight abilities rival
those of Iron Man.

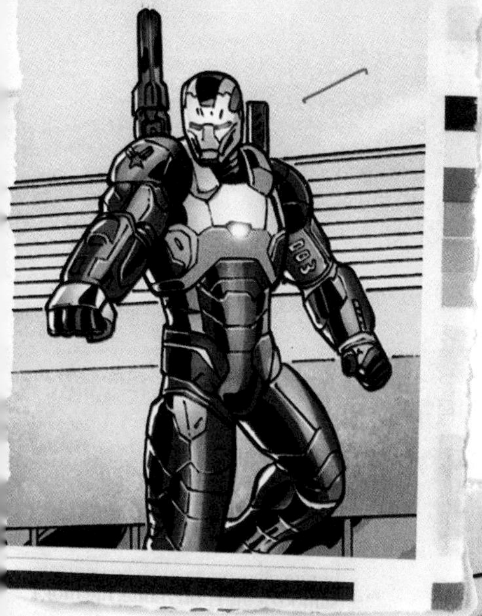

His experience in the field should not be underestimated.

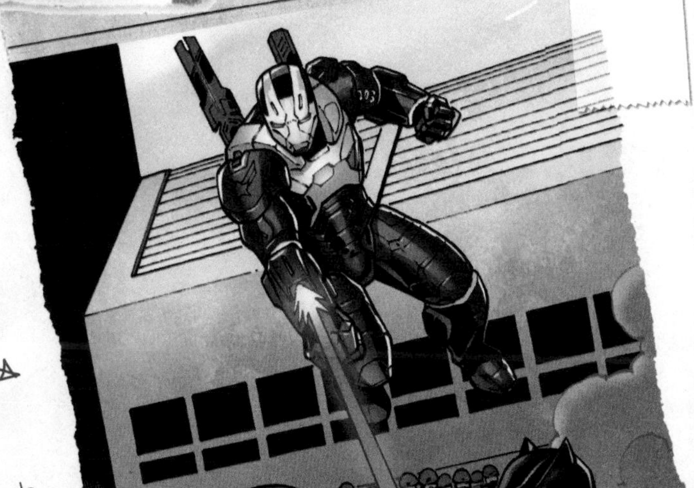

War Machine excels at crowd control, even among powerful combatants.

STRATEGIC HOMELAND INTERVENTION ENFORCEMENT LOGISTICS DIVISION

80

S.H.I.E.L.D.

Strategic Homeland Intervention, Enforcement and Logistics Division—more commonly referred to as S.H.I.E.L.D.—was responsible for safeguarding the world from enormous threats, focusing on espionage, global politics, and superhuman activity. After it was revealed that the villainous Hydra organization had infiltrated S.H.I.E.L.D.'s highest ranks, the department was largely disbanded.

CONFIDENTIAL

S.H.I.E.L.D. HISTORY

Howard Stark and Peggy Carter originally founded S.H.I.E.L.D. in the wake of World War II. Their goal was to protect the United States, and later the world, from any threat imaginable.

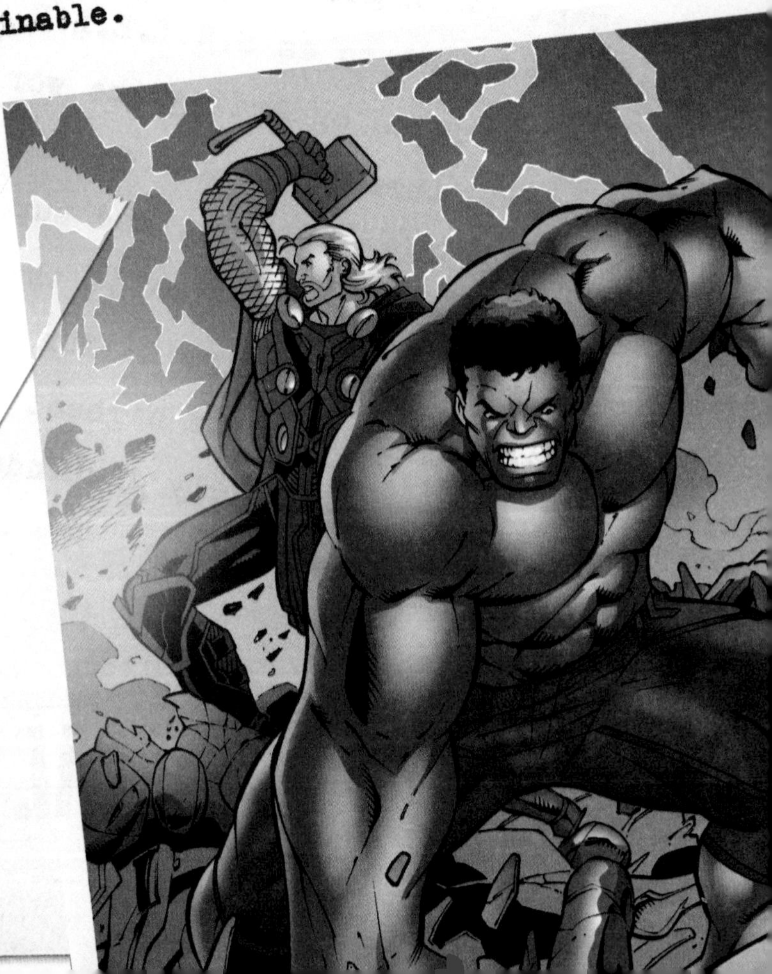

Eventually run by Nick Fury with help from Deputy Director Maria Hill, S.H.I.E.L.D. had a direct hand in the formation of the super team known as the Avengers.

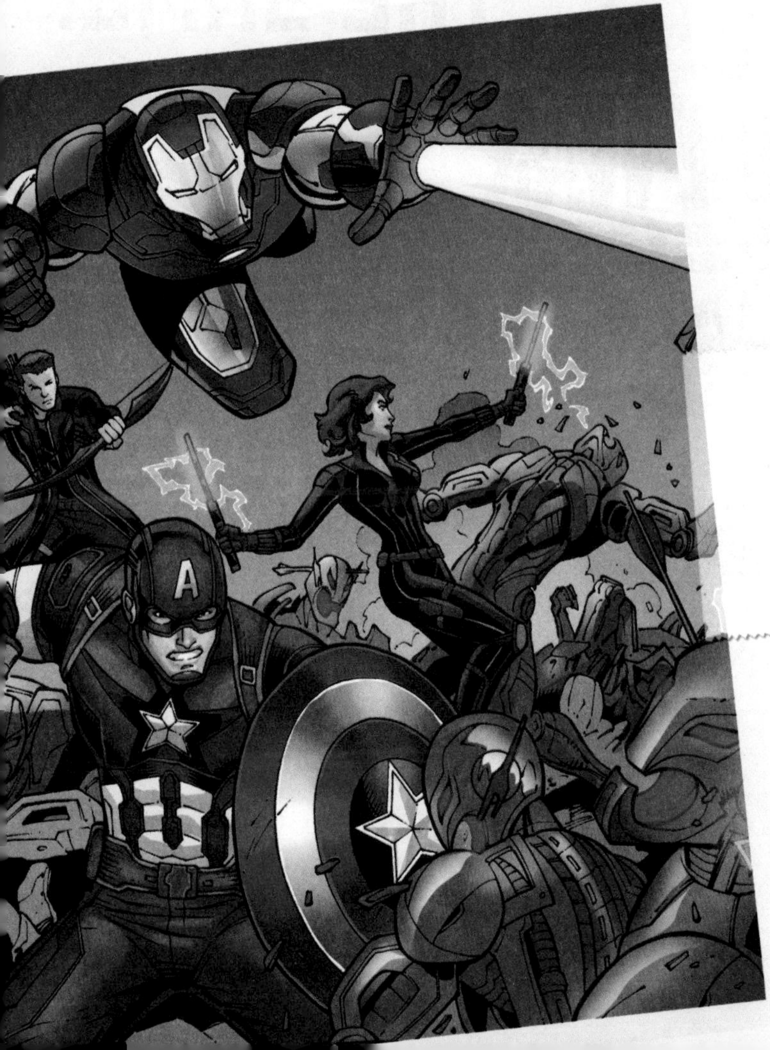

MARVEL
CIVIL WAR
CAPTAIN AMERICA
INCLUDES POSTER!
CAPTAIN AMERICA
VERSUS
IRON MAN
FLIP THE BOOK TO CHOOSE A SIDE!

MARVEL
CIVIL WAR
CAPTAIN AMERICA
THE RISE OF
CROSSBONES
BASED ON THE MOVIE!

MARVEL
CIVIL WAR
CAPTAIN AMERICA
PASSPORT 2 READING
WE ARE THE AVENGERS
BASED ON THE MOVIE!

MARVEL
CIVIL WAR
CAPTAIN AMERICA
PASSPORT 2 READING
ESCAPE FROM BLACK PANTHER

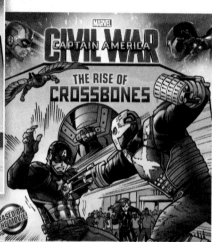

RELIVE THE EXCITEMENT
THE MARVEL CINEMATIC UNIVERSE
BEGINS HERE

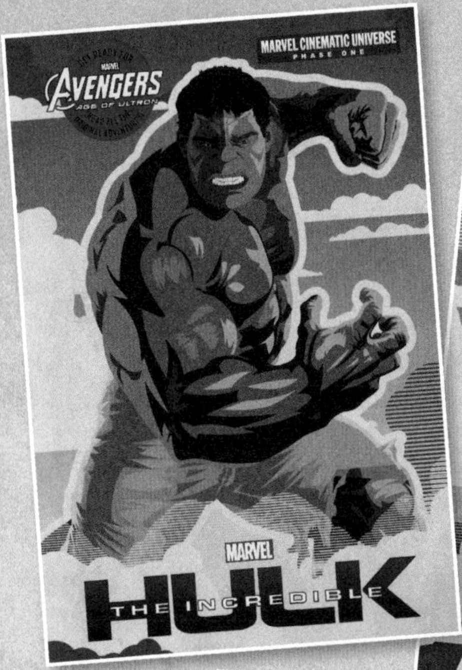
MARVEL CINEMATIC UNIVERSE
PHASE ONE
AVENGERS
AGE OF ULTRON
MARVEL
THE INCREDIBLE HULK

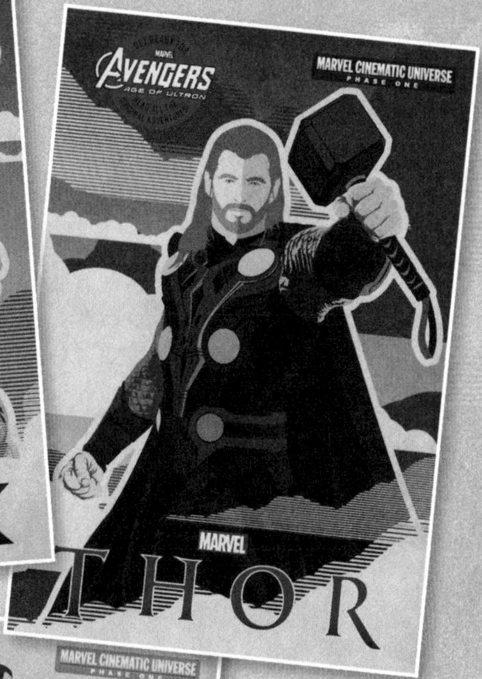
AVENGERS
AGE OF ULTRON
MARVEL CINEMATIC UNIVERSE
PHASE ONE
MARVEL
THOR

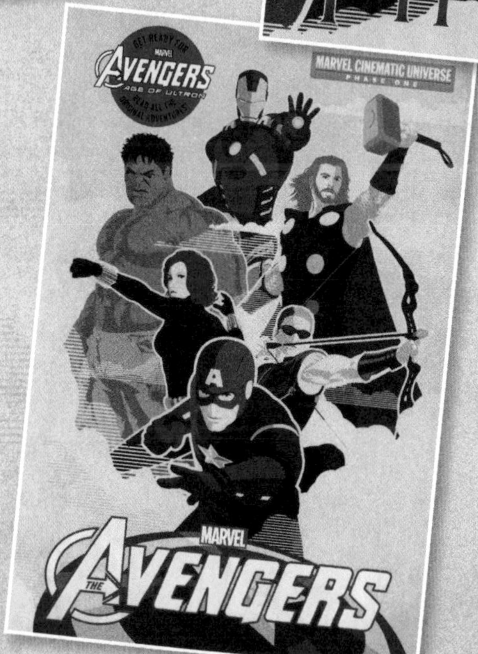
GET READY FOR
MARVEL
AVENGERS
AGE OF ULTRON
READ ALL THE
ORIGINAL ADVENTURES!
MARVEL CINEMATIC UNIVERSE
PHASE ONE
MARVEL
THE AVENGERS

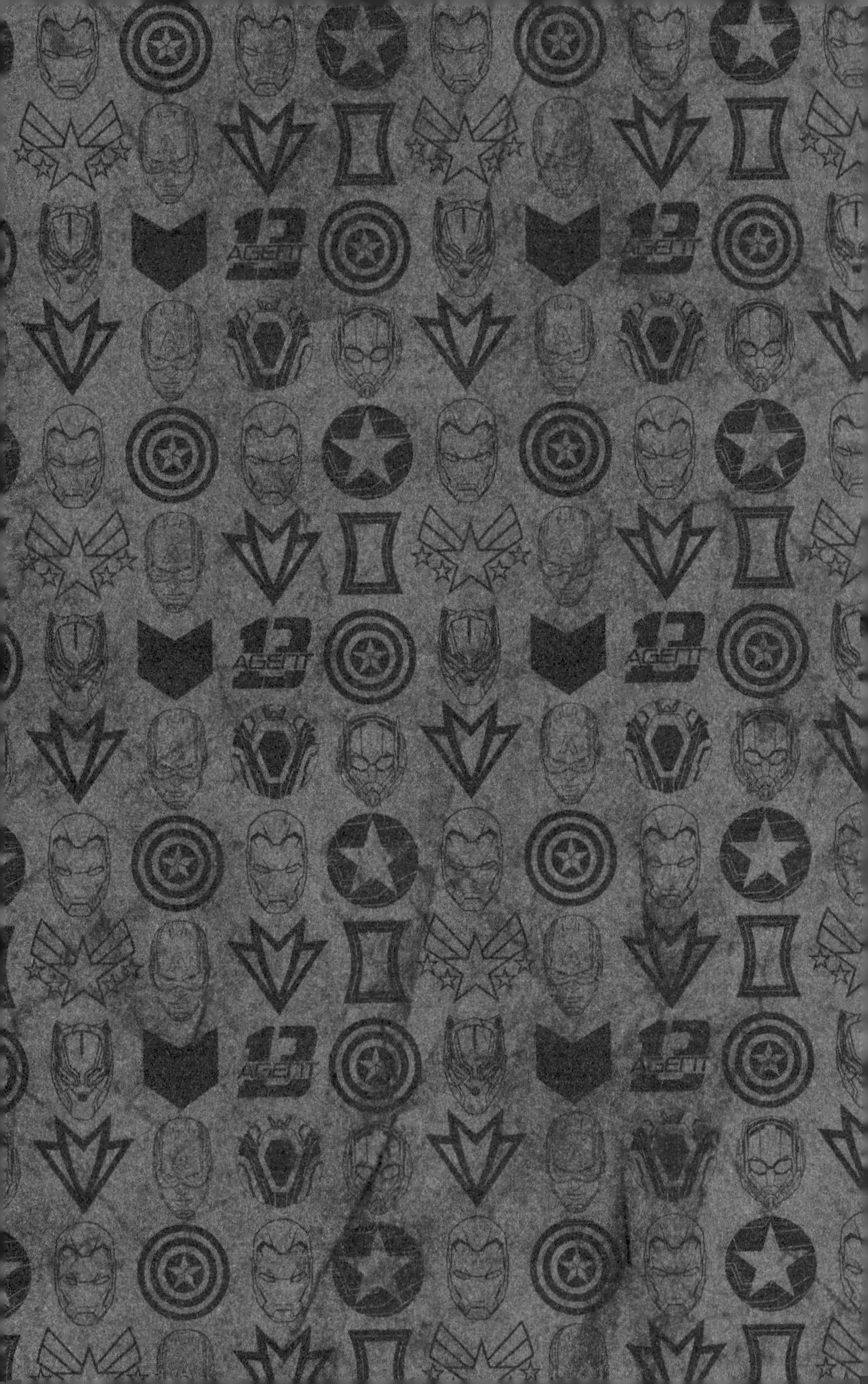

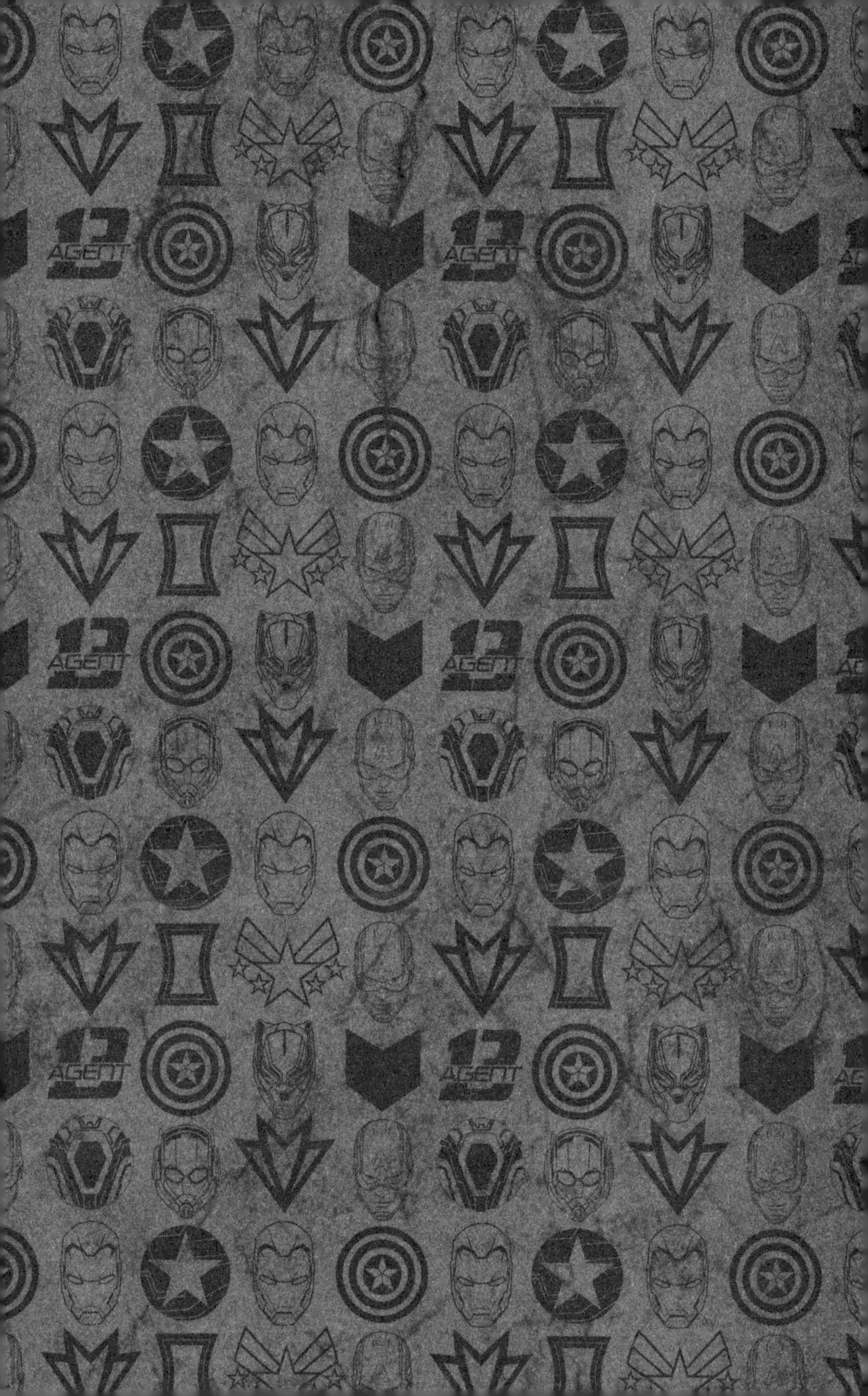